JUSTICE at PEACHTREE

JUSTICE at PEACHTREE

Mary Ann Marger

ELSEVIER/NELSON BOOKS
New York

No character in this book is intended to
represent any actual person; all the incidents of the
story are entirely fictional in nature.

Mary Ann Marger

Library of Congress Cataloging in Publication Data

Marger, Mary Ann.
Justice at Peachtree.

SUMMARY: When Cary Bowen takes a job with her
father's newspaper during the last year of high school,
she becomes more aware of the racial prejudice in her
small town of Peachtree, South Carolina in 1950.
[1. Race relations—Fiction.   2. Prejudices—Fiction.
3. City and town life—Fiction.
4. Journalism—Fiction.]   I. Title.
PZ7.M33545Ju   [Fic]   80-18639
ISBN 0-525-66690-7

Published in the United States by Elsevier/Nelson Books,
a division of Elsevier-Dutton Publishing Company, Inc.,
New York. Published simultaneously in Don Mills,
Ontario, by Nelson /Canada.
Printed in the U.S.A.
First Edition
10 9 8 7 6 5 4 3 2 1

ACKNOWLEDGMENTS

The author expresses sincere appreciation to those who helped with this book: her parents, Herman and Theresa T. Baum; Helen Breeland, Charleston, SC; Norma Lewis, St. Petersburg, FL; Honorable Paul H. Roney, Judge, U.S. Fifth Circuit Court of Appeals; and the staff of the St. Petersburg (FL) Public Library.

To my husband and children,
Bruce, Bill, David, and Susan

JUSTICE at
PEACHTREE

one

Except for Gaston Wells, whom I really couldn't count, Armand Larue was my first boyfriend. And now I'd lost him, just for doing what I thought was right.

I sat on the ground, leaned my back against the willow tree, and pondered the events that had brought me to my current dismal state. We'd been to the end-of-the-year junior-class beach party out at the pond. I'd slathered myself with suntan lotion and worked on what was already a pretty good tan. I'd felt warm and glowing inside as well as out. Armand's presence on the towel by my side had made me the envy of every other girl at Peachtree High School. Ahead of me stretched the whole three months of the summer of 1950, and I had intended to spend most of it right at the beach, sunning, swimming, picnicking and, of course, admiring this gorgeous, muscle-bound guy who would be captain and quarter-back of our football team next fall. Armand was all I needed to make my senior year a success.

I hadn't questioned why he'd fallen for me. It certainly wasn't for my looks. I was too skinny, my brown hair was too curly, and I never could seem to pull my clothes together right.

Occasionally I would raise my head from the beach towel to see what Gaston was doing. He kept pretty much to himself, swimming back and forth to the float, or sitting by a tree sipping a Coke, or playing with a twig in the sand. Only recently had his height passed mine and his voice grown husky. I had hoped his new maturity might encourage him to date someone else. Why did he expect me to be always there for him, just because I lived next door? We were the same age, and like almost every-body in Peachtree, South Carolina, we had never lived anywhere else. Gaston and I both lived in the houses our grandparents had been born in. We'd been best friends all our lives, even through grade school, when boys aren't supposed to like girls.

But now we were getting older. It was time for us to be establishing other relationships. He would just have to learn that he couldn't depend on me for company any-more. I turned back to Armand, who nuzzled my nose. I giggled.

The afternoon went quickly. We were among the last to leave. I shook out the beach towels and we piled our things into Armand's jalopy. We rode into town, past Wells' Department Store, past the Confederate War Memorial at Broad and Lafayette streets, then four blocks to Magnolia, the dirt road on which I lived, past Judge Westbrook's old Victorian house on the corner, then past Gaston's house to mine. We pulled up in front.

I hopped out of the car, ran up on the porch, and tried the doorknob. It was locked. I rang the bell. I knew it was too early for Mom, Dad, or Uncle Jasper to be home, but Annie, the maid, should be answering. Unless . . . darn. I remembered that Annie was taking the afternoon off.

"What's the matter, Cary?" asked Armand, who had followed me up the steps. "Can't get in?"

I thought for a minute. "Yes, I can. The back door will be locked, too, but there's another way."

We walked down the driveway, which was encrusted with pebbles, dirt, and weeds, to the rear of the house. There, behind a crumbling brick wall that sheltered the garbage cans, set back beyond the camouflaging cover of a weeping willow, was a wooden door that badly needed a coat of varnish. The bottom hinge was off, and the jamb was so tight at the top that a thief would have thought it locked. But I knew that if I turned the rusty knob, put my free hand against the wall, and pulled hard, it would give.

"Well, I'll be," said Armand from behind me as the door opened, revealing pitch-blackness inside. At our feet was the beginning of a staircase. "Where does that go?"

"It's my secret stairway," I said, faking a cryptic air. "Follow those stairs and you'll find all the ghosts of Peachtree."

Armand's eyes widened, which surprised me, since I figured he was too old for ghost stories. But soon he regained his composure and asked, "Aw, c'mon, what are those stairs doing here?"

I figured I might as well explain. "Oh, it's just an old

staircase the slaves used to use when they entered the house from their quarters in the backyard. The slave quarters were torn down long ago, and even Annie doesn't use this entrance now. I don't blame her. It's so dark. There isn't a light or a window or even a railing. I guess the slaves just had to feel their way along. Anyway, nowadays it sure comes in handy when I'm locked out."

Armand's hands were on either side of the doorframe now, and though his feet were still on the ground outside, his stance forced me just inside the threshold. In the dark, musty stairwell I felt a slight fear, which I attributed to all the spooky tales Gaston and I had conjured up when we played here as children. "Those stairs sure are dark," said Armand. "I can just barely make 'em out."

He gently pushed me farther in. "Hmmm. This bears looking into." His eyes seemed to follow the stairwell, but his hand was roving underneath my beach jacket and had begun to fiddle with the hook on the back of my bathing suit.

"Armand Larue, cut that out!" I snapped, turning and facing him.

"Ah, come on," he said, "We're past the third date."

"Not that far past!" I shrieked, and lunged forward at him, with both hands in front of me. My sudden movement against his chest caught him unprepared. He tumbled out of the door and fell backward onto the ground. As he stared at me in amazement, I sputtered, "I'm sorry! I didn't mean to hurt you!"

"You didn't," he said in disgust, picking himself up and dusting off his jeans, "I'm just glad to find out now what kind of girl you are, instead of wasting any more time on you. First you give me this bull about waiting until our third date for a kiss. One kiss and that's it, huh? You're too cold for me!" He started walking down the driveway. I followed him a short distance until he turned and shot back, "Yes, I sure am glad I found out now. Besides, the way you sit out in the sun all the time, somebody might think I was taking out a nigger. Yes sirree, I sure am glad."

I wanted to run after him and say, "Wait! I didn't mean it!" but something kept me from going farther. Maybe it was my revulsion at hearing him refer to me by a word I wasn't allowed even to use. Maybe it was just my own pride.

Once I heard his car drive off, I sat down beneath the willow and mulled over the change in my fate. I knew fast girls could have almost any man they wanted temporarily, but in the end, so I'd heard, they'd lose not only their reputations. Maybe Armand would realize I was different and come back.

On that dim hope, I climbed the darkened flight of stairs. The door on the first landing opened into the laundry room. A table there was piled with freshly washed and ironed clothes, ready to be put away. I walked into the kitchen, where three pots stood on the stove. One contained gumbo, another, sieva beans, and the third, water only, for the rice became gummy if cooked too far ahead of time. In the refrigerator was a pitcher of iced tea and a bowl of date pudding. I smelled fried chicken. Annie had done a good day's work before she left.

The chicken lay on a platter, alongside three serving bowls for the vegetables, in the butler's pantry between the kitchen and the dining room. I picked up a wing and began chewing on it as I walked on. The dinner table was covered with a fresh cloth embroidered by my aunt in

Charleston, and the four places were set with the silver and what was left of the fine china that had been used in my father's family every evening for generations. Our napkins were neatly rolled and placed in engraved silver rings.

I turned on the fan so the room would be cool and comfortable for our meal. Annie certainly was amazing, managing both our house and hers, what with nine kids of her own and no husband. And she made the world's best fried chicken. I wondered if the family would miss another wing, or if all this food going to my stomach would satisfy my broken heart.

I was determined to hide my unhappiness at dinner, but nobody would have even noticed it. There was unhappiness enough. Dad had brought the bookkeeping records home from *The Peachtree News* for Uncle Jasper to review. Dad knew already, though, that Uncle Jasper's auditing would reveal no surprises. The weekly newspaper that provided the family livelihood had been losing advertisers steadily. More and more, the larger companies in our town were turning to the Charleston *News and Courier* for their advertising. Charleston was fifty miles away, and the paper was delivered daily to most of the people in Peachtree. Its rates were not much higher than the level to which Dad had been forced to raise his. Our circulation was down, too. No new industry had come to town for some time. Old Peachtree families occasionally moved away in search of more progressive communities. In fact, all our family had either died or left, except for us.

Uncle Jasper spoke. "I'll just go to Garth Wells and ask him for a raise. I'll check and see when was the last time he gave me one. It must be five years."

I wondered if Uncle Jasper really could check. His

office on the balcony of Gaston's dad's store was the messiest place I'd ever seen. Stacks of old, worn ledger books were piled high on tables along the back wall and side partitions. Uncle Jasper's whole forty years' worth of bookkeeping for Wells' Department Store looked as though it had never been dusted or even moved. Uncle Jasper seemed to spend all his time sitting in his swivel chair, his back to his rolltop desk, entertaining his cronies who came to visit throughout each day. I wondered why Mr. Wells paid him as much as he did. Still, I loved and respected my uncle, as did everyone else in town, including Mr. Wells.

"There are other solutions," said Mother. "Maybe we should consider letting Annie go."

"You can't do that!" I cried. "You can't just turn her out when she has nine kids to feed. You know jobs are hard to come by for colored people. Besides, she's been here so long she's like a member of the family."

But Mother continued, "She's a good maid. She won't have any trouble. Maybe she can even find a place where she'll get more than the eleven dollars a week we pay her."

My mind was clicking quickly. Annie had been with the family since she was thirteen. She might not be able to adapt to another situation. I voiced another solution as I was thinking it. "Maybe I could get a job over the summer. After all, I am seventeen. Maybe Mr. Wells would hire me."

Dad nodded approval. "I'm sure he would. You ought to make enough so we could pay Annie and you could buy your school needs for the fall. That would help us for the next few months. Then we can review the situation again. Of course, Cary, it won't leave you much time for yourself. Or for the Larue boy."

I grimaced. Then in a slow, even voice I announced,

"In the future, you may refer to the Larue boy in the past tense."

"Good riddance," said Mother. She'd never approved of Armand anyway. Unconsciously, she reached for the dinner bell, which had been placed on the sideboard instead of in its usual position, when Annie was there, near Mother's glass. She withdrew her hand to her lap. "Cary, will you serve dessert?"

"Yes, ma'am," I said, gathering up the dinner plates to take out to the kitchen.

I wondered which would be the better time to approach Mr. Wells: tomorrow, my first day of vacation, or tonight, while he was out on our front porch. If I talked to him tonight, I could start work in the morning.

A job would be good for me, in more ways than helping the family out of a bind. Considering my record with the male sex, I had to face the prospect that I might never marry, and I had better learn a marketable skill. I'd always dreamed of being a writer and probably running *The Peachtree News* when Dad retired, but now the newspaper couldn't be relied on for a living wage.

When the last clean pot had been dried and put away, I walked out to where the men were gathered. Watching the twilight drift into darkness on our front porch was a summer ritual for the men of my family's acquaintance. The road was little traveled, and the dusk was slow in setting in, bringing a gratifying breeze to ease away the day's heat. Uncle Jasper and Mr. Wells were always there, as was Dad. The other members varied, and from time to time included any of the men who lived within walking distance, except Judge Westbrook.

On this particular evening the three regulars had assembled, and Gaston was sitting off to one side. He looked up and beamed as I pushed open the screen door. Dad must have told him about Armand already.

Mr. Wells glanced in my direction, too. "Hear you're looking for summer employment, young lady."

Darn it, I thought. Couldn't I apply for the job myself? How was I ever going to make it in the working world if I couldn't learn to do things on my own?

"Don't look so glum," said Uncle Jasper, "Salesladies need to wear big smiles and be pleasant."

Mr. Wells said, "I could use somebody in notions. Do you know the difference between size-eight thread and size-fifty? Or worsted yarn from sports? You'll learn. I pay three dollars a day starting out, before deductions. That's for five and a half days; the store closes Wednesday afternoons, of course."

"Yes, sir," I said.

Gaston grinned, "I'll be working there, too, in men's wear."

I looked away, saying nothing. It could have been an uncomfortable moment, except that everyone else on the porch had suddenly grown quiet, too. They were staring down the road toward Broad Street where old Judge Westbrook and his second wife, some twenty years younger than he, were just leaving the side entrance of their house for an evening walk. They strolled up Magnolia, past the Wellses' house, then were even with ours, then went on into the gathering darkness. No word of greeting was exchanged, no nod or smile or friendly wave. The judge and his wife bore straight ahead, and the men on the porch watched in stony silence. Only after the pair had passed a considerable distance did Mr. Wells speak in a low voice, "That durn fool of a judge, he's turned crazy as a coot."

two

Once I learned a few facts about pins, threads, patterns, and special gadgets for attaching snaps or counting knitting rows, my life at the notions counter of Wells' Department Store settled into a busy routine. By July I was even ready to offer advice. I deftly and quickly flipped to the proper pages of the McCall's and Simplicity pattern books for two women hunting apron patterns to make for a church bazaar. As the women discussed choices, I spotted Mrs. Westbrook several aisles away, at the cosmetics counter.

One of the women had seen her, too. She turned back to the books as she said to her companion, "Don't look now, but the judge's wife just came in. She's over in cosmetics, trying on face paint."

"I wouldn't debase myself to look around at her," said the other woman. "As far as I'm concerned she doesn't exist. I can't tell you how often I think of the shame, the humiliation of that poor first wife, and what she must be going through in Charleston. Imagine, at her age, having to leave the town where she's always lived, all because of her husband's scandalous action. I tell you, we'll all rue the day they legalized divorce in South Carolina two years ago."

"And remember how quickly the judge took advantage of it!" said the first woman, "Like he'd been waiting for years. And then he has the nerve to up and marry that hussy from Boston. Did you know that in the General Assembly in Columbia our legislators are arguing for his impeachment?"

"You don't say! Because he married that woman?"

"Oh, no. They can't impeach him because of that, as long as she's white. It's because of the decision he made right afterward, the one saying colored folks had a right to vote in the state primary election when we choose our Democratic candidates."

"But none of the colored voted, not in Peachtree at least."

"Not two years ago, but do you know he's agitating about it again? He's announced that at next Tuesday's election, he'll be sitting in the federal courthouse, ready to try anybody who's interfering with colored people's voting rights."

"But we've always had a white primary. He has no right to change that. It's the law."

"Yes, but it's state law, not federal. And he's a federal judge. He claims South Carolina has to obey the amendment to the United States Constitution that gave colored people the right to vote, and just voting in the general election isn't enough."

"I don't even like to think about it," the other woman said, turning back to her pattern book. "Look at this darling cobbler's apron, dear. It has pockets across the front, and the pattern is all in one piece. We could whip it up in a hurry."

The ladies bought that pattern and one for a tea apron. I helped them pick out several fabrics, matching thread, and contrasting trim. I was learning a lot about sewing, though the thought of a future spent making aprons for church bazaars filled me with gloom. I'd rather, I resolved, go through life selling notions at Wells'. During the five weeks I'd been there, almost everyone in town had passed through, and I was learning a great deal about human nature just by listening and observing.

One person I didn't need to learn about, and hadn't expected to see in my department, was Armand. But there he was, the morning of Election Day, walking arm in arm with Sugar Moran.

Gaston had told me he'd seen Armand with Sugar. I'd hoped he was just saying that to make me think more kindly toward himself. But now I could see it was true. They flipped through a knitting book of men's sweaters; at least, Sugar did. Armand was so absorbed in her that he hardly looked at the book. Neither even acted as though they had seen me.

I soothed my injured pride by telling myself that it wouldn't last, not with Sugar's background being what it was. She was pretty, and always seemed surrounded by the cutest boys in the school. She got along well with the girls, too, even though everyone knew her family was just poor white trash. She lived in a shack on the edge of what had once been a cotton plantation owned by my family. It had been the home of sharecroppers who had long since left, now that the land was turned to pasture. In my limited association with Sugar, I'd always found her fun to talk to, but she wasn't someone I'd want for a close friend.

Armand and Sugar didn't buy anything. She put back the book, in the wrong place so I had to follow them and rearrange it, and they walked off together.

At quitting time Uncle Jasper and Gaston met me as usual at the front door of the store so we could walk home together. But this evening Uncle Jasper asked if we wouldn't mind stopping off at the polls so he could vote. Gaston and I had never been to a polling place, and Uncle Jasper thought it might add to our knowledge of government. We learned more than government by arriving when we did.

The polls were at the courthouse, on the corner of Lafayette and Broad streets. We walked up the steps, past a marshal who nodded cordially, and into the spacious lobby ringed by a balcony. A long table stretched part of the way across the back of the room. Behind it sat two townsmen, with open books in front of them. Two official-looking men were positioned around the room, and a woman stood at a high table, marking a paper ballot.

Uncle Jasper voted quickly and was about to leave when another person entered the room: Willis. Willis was a tall, gray-haired, bent-over black man, a handyman, a jack-of-all-trades. In all my life I'd never seen him wear anything but a white, rumpled, collarless shirt and a pair of baggy, tattered, gray pants, held up by suspenders. Often I'd hear Annie yell out the back door, "Willis! Come here!" and he seemed invariably to be within earshot. He did the sort of jobs around the neighborhood that everyone else was either too weak or too lazy to do, such as cleaning the second-floor windows or fixing the septic tank when I couldn't stand to come within fifty feet of it. We'd always give him a dollar or two, which he usually turned over to the church. He existed on food that Annie otherwise would have thrown out: blood-spotted eggs, bruised and wilted vegetables, and leftovers just beginning to spoil. In spite of his diet he was never sick, a fact my father attributed to the natural penicillin in mold.

And here was Willis, as unlikely a person as I could imagine, about to vote in the white primary election. He walked just inside the door and paused beneath a clock on the balcony. Slowly he removed his hat. He looked around and made a little bow toward each official. Then he walked forward, pausing where we stood in the middle of the floor. He bowed again and said, "Evenin', Mr. Bowen, Miss Cary, Master Gaston."

"Good evening, Willis," each of us whispered, as though we were afraid for the others in the room to hear us. We always called Negroes by their first name and they always addressed us with a title, regardless of our age.

Willis continued ahead, slowly, with all eyes upon him. He stepped up to the table and waited for one of the white men to speak first.

The man looked at him beneath a fixed brow. "Hey, what you doin' here, nigger?"

Willis answered, "I come to vote."

The man straightened up and faced the table squarely. He flipped through the registration book. "You got proof of payin' your poll tax in the general elections?"

"Yas, suh."

"Then show it."

Uncle Jasper hadn't had to show any proof, I thought. He just walked right up, received his ballot, and walked away.

Willis pulled some neatly folded papers from his shirt pocket, receipts accumulated from every general election in which he had voted.

"C'mon," said the white man, "all of 'em."

Willis felt in his pocket. "I done give you all of 'em, suh. They's all right there."

The man spent some time going over them, and then muttered, "They seem to be in order." He then reached for a small book on the desk, opened it, and pointed to a passage. "Read this, boy, and tell me what it means. Can't have no uneducated people voting, can we?"

"No, suh," answered Willis. I waited, expecting to hear the halting, disjointed sounds of one who has not learned to read well. But he surprised me by reading smoothly the section of the Constitution that tells how it can be amended. The man then asked for an interpretation, which Willis was able to give. At last he was handed his ballot. He said, "Thank you, suh," made a little bow, and went to one of the tall tables to mark it.

I took a long, deep breath, as though I'd been afraid to inhale the whole time Willis had been there. We later found out that two other Negroes had voted during the day. The poll workers were certain they had been hand-picked and coached by Judge Westbrook.

"I thought poll taxes and education tests were illegal," I said as we walked home.

"Not yet," said Uncle Jasper, "There's a movement toward it, but the law hasn't been changed yet."

"What amazed me," said Gaston, "was that Willis could read."

"We learned to read together," explained Uncle Jasper. "His parents were born slaves of the Bowen family, and when they were freed, they just stayed right on working for us. Of course, he was born a free man in 1883, same year as me. Back in those days it wasn't uncommon for a white child to have a Negro boy go to school with him to carry his books and lunch. Willis and I studied together and we learned together. I was the brightest boy in the class, and Judge Westbrook was second. I suspect Willis might have been third, if he hadn't had to quit to go work in the fields. But then, he'd have quit by 1896 anyway."

"Why?" asked Gaston. "What happened then?"

"South Carolina enforced a law that said colored and white children couldn't attend the same school. Of course, that was with the understanding that colored schools would be equal to white schools. At the time, Peachtree didn't even have a place it could call a colored school, and the first place they did have was mighty inferior."

I was envious. Uncle Jasper had at one time known a black person as an equal, in a way that I never could. Half the people who lived in and around Peachtree were Negro, yet I knew not one of them, not even Annie, really well. I said to Uncle Jasper, "I guess you're mighty glad to see Willis finally getting a voice in government."

"Heck, no," replied Uncle Jasper. "Willis' vote ain't going to change the outcome any. And while I don't deny him the right to vote, I do have a bone to pick with the way it came about."

"What do you mean?"

"I guess you're too young to see, child, it's Judge Westbrook's way of getting revenge. He's been ostracized from society for marrying that damn Yankee wife of his. He's been made to resign from my club, and lost all his friends, even me, as you well know. Why, Gaston, your dad even closed up his charge account at the store.Yep, the judge is just getting even for the way he's been treated. I can't say I blame him for that, but I sure don't understand how a man can change so much."

I wondered, too. When I was a child and he was married to his first wife, I'd visited his home often. He had always acted very kindly toward me.

"You don't think he's just changed his way of thinking?" I asked. "Could it be that his wife has made him regard colored people the same way as they are up North?"

"Nope," replied Uncle Jasper. "I've known the judge all my life, and he's never had a liberal thought in his head. And now all of a sudden he starts spouting this stuff about it being time South Carolina rejoined the Union. I tell you, Cary, it's revenge. Of course, Gaston, your dad would disagree. He thinks the judge is just plain crazy."

We were all at our house now, and Uncle Jasper started up the stairs of the front porch, huffing and snorting at each pace. He didn't notice that Gaston and I were still standing at the bottom.

"Do you suppose that's true about your uncle being smarter than Judge Westbrook?" asked Gaston.

"Oh, it's true," I replied. "You know how Uncle Jasper often talks about the great classics of literature, and how he solves mathematical problems in his head. He majored in Greek at an Ivy League school. Dad says he graduated first in his class there."

"But what did he ever do with all that book learning? I mean, in the way of making money."

"Dad says he never reckoned that was important. I guess he just figured he'd come back to Peachtree, work for your grandfather and then for your father. Maybe he'll be your bookkeeper someday, Gaston."

"I guess so," said Gaston.

Uncle Jasper was my grandfather's youngest and only surviving brother. But he was sixty-seven, and he couldn't live forever. Besides, wasn't he entitled to a few years of retirement?

That's how things were in Peachtree. The only changes were brought about by deaths, births, and marriages. And sometimes you forgot about them, and expected everything to remain forever just as it was today.

three

Summer passed quickly. The days when I didn't work were spent at the pond with Gaston, not by choice, but by convenience. Most girls had a close female friend to confide in, but I always had Gaston. And anyway, at my age it was more prestigious to be seen in public with a member of the opposite sex.

Everyone always thought Gaston and I would eventually marry each other, though we had never discussed it. Everyone except Mother. She nursed the dream that after graduation I would go off to Syracuse University in New York and fall madly in love with a dashing and brilliant student destined for success. Mom was from Syracuse, and that was where she had met Dad, who had somehow wound up there, studying journalism. His own dream was to leave Peachtree and pursue a newspaper or writing career in New York City, which was, to him, the ultimate place for an aspiring writer to live. But he graduated from college just as the Depression hit, and he could not find a job. His dream ended when he came back home.

In all my life I had been to Syracuse only once, with Mother when I was five. Her side of the family came to visit us every second or third Christmas, and they all commented about how my mother had become a real Southerner. But the people in Peachtree didn't consider her a Southerner at all, because she'd been born north of the Mason-Dixon line. She never complained, but I knew she had never been asked to join the women's club, to which the real society in Peachtree, and my father's mother when she was alive, belonged.

With summer's end came school. I continued to work at the store on Saturdays, the busiest day of the week. Mr. Wells moved me to ladies' dresses, saying it was good experience to learn about the different departments. He moved Gaston to the shoe department, just across the main aisle from me.

I hoped that my working would prevent Dad from thinking any more about the family economy. In fact, the only time the subject arose he bluntly said he needed something of a miracle to keep *The Peachtree News* in business much longer, the way things were going.

I took a heavy load of academic courses. Solid geometry was a high point of each day only because Armand Larue sat behind me. He might be going steady with Sugar, but I still believed it was only a matter of time till he'd be looking for someone else. I secretly hoped that if I were slow and steady I might meet Armand at the finish line yet. I melted every time he tapped me on the shoulder and whispered, "Tell me again the formula for the volume of a sphere."

My favorite subject, though, was United States government, because it was taught by my favorite teacher, Miss Celia Callaway. Miss Callaway was the hardest, the strictest, and the meanest teacher in the school. But we learned.

There was another reason for my lavishing so much admiration on her. She was faculty adviser for the school newspaper, *The Red and Gold*, named for our school colors. The paper was the best in its category in the state. We had taken first place three times in the last five years at the Scholastic Press Association conventions.

I was managing editor in name only. Miss Callaway did all the managing and all the editing. Even Joe Gibbs, the lanky, pop-eyed editor in chief, followed her dictates on subjects for editorials. Nobody seemed to mind.

One day I stayed after school to help Joe crank out the first issue on the ornery mimeograph machine, and decided, just for fun, to enter the house through the secret stairway. As I opened the door to the laundry room, I heard a strange yet pleasing sound flow out from the kitchen. I put my books on the ironing board and tiptoed in to investigate.

It was Annie. Her back was to me, and she was doing a little dance, moving her feet in short steps and fluttering her hands at waist height. The words were half hummed, half spoken in an unfamiliar dialect. She was totally engrossed in her performance, and I dared not move. All too soon she spun around to face me, causing an abrupt halt to both mood and movement as her face froze in a somber expression. She walked over to the stove and began stirring a stew in a pot.

"Don't stop because of me," I pleaded, "I like your dance. Please go on."

It was no use. She wouldn't even talk about it. That was Annie's way. She would discuss anything concerning the house, or indulge in moderate gossip about the people who frequented it, but her own life was sealed off and private. Was she ashamed of it? Did she think I wasn't interested? Oh, but I was. Even her own children came around so seldom I hardly recognized them. They grew so much in between visits.

Of all of them, I knew only her third child, second son. He had come to our house one day because he had a bad cut on his finger and his sister, left in charge, couldn't stop the bleeding. I was nine at the time, the sister was eight, and the boy was six. I had watched Annie quickly treat and wrap the wound and chastise the boy for interrupting her work. When she was finished she said, "Aren't you going to say hello to Miss Cary?"

The boy just looked at me with a shy smile, his feet rooted to the linoleum floor, his body pivoting slowly around, back and forth.

"What's your name?" I asked.

No answer.

"Didn't you hear Miss Cary?" asked Annie, impatiently. "She ask you what yo' name is. Tell her."

The boy answered, "Ra'."

"You know yo' name's more'n that. Tell Miss Cary yo' whole name."

The boy hesitated, then said, "Ra' Ruh-fuh."

Annie sighed. "Yo' whole name's Ralph Rutherford Brown. Now, why you not tell Miss Cary?"

Ralph continued to twist, and now his mouth puckered into a quivering pout.

"Go run along home," said Annie. "I got no time for foolishness. I got work to do."

Ralph opened the back door, walked down the stairs, skipped across our yard, through the fence, and started down the long, worn, yellow clay road that led through the field behind our property. I followed him in a surge of curiosity.

As I reached the fence I called, "Ralph."

The boy turned and waited to see what I had in mind.

"You want to play a game?" I asked, wondering what activity we might know in common.

Without a word, Ralph came nearer, reached in his pocket, and pulled out a small, grubby sack of marbles. He gently eased them out and onto the ground. Then, with his big toe, he drew a circle. He stood back to see if I approved,then counted out and shoved half the marbles to me, and sat on his haunches waiting for my move.

We played perhaps twenty minutes. The only sounds Ralph made were an occasional giggle or an exclamation of pleasure or dismay at his own shot. When I knew I had to quit and go home the marbles were fairly evenly divided. He waited to see if I planned to keep mine. But I moved quickly to dispel any fear over what must have been one of his few possessions. "Here," I said, picking up the sack and placing my marbles inside, "They were yours when we started. They're still yours now."

Ralph grinned, stuffed the sack back in his pocket, and ran down the road to his home.

I never played with Ralph again, but in the years that followed, Ralph always had a big smile for me. We shared something, even if neither of us knew what that something was.

Not long after the day I interrupted Annie's dance, we had our first cold snap, forcing the evening conversation group to move indoors to the parlor. It must have been a Thursday, because Uncle Jasper was reading aloud from *The Peachtree News*, which Mother had brought home. Dad hadn't come home with her. Mother said something about his working late, which was unusual. Normally the arrival of the paper meant my parents had done their job for the week and could take the next few days a bit easier.

Uncle Jasper's audience included Mr. Wells and J.T. Larue, Armand's dad. I didn't much care for Mr. Larue, because he was always arguing with the others, but I had to admit he did make the conversations more lively. Mr. Larue's brother was the chief of police, a position which he said gave him an insight on the Negro race that none of the rest of us could have.

"There's a new high school over in Maryville," said Uncle Jasper, peering at the newspaper through the bottom part of his glasses.

"A nigger school," said Mr. Larue.

The mention of the word "Maryville" raised hatred in me, for they were our archrivals in football. But a new Negro school posed no threat, since black and white teams never played each other.

"They've named it Washington High. It looks right pretty from the picture," Uncle Jasper continued, "thirteen classrooms, but no library or athletic facilities."

"They don't need none," muttered Mr. Larue, "They wouldn't know what to do with them things if they had 'em. Still, your nephew oughta have more sense than to mention that in the newspaper. Some cockeyed liberal is going to get the idea the school ain't equal to Maryville High, and make a big fuss about it."

Uncle Jasper put the paper aside. "Things are changing, you know," he said, "There's all kinds of court decisions these days favoring Negroes. Legally, colored people have a lot of rights. They just don't use them."

"And they ain't gonna use 'em," answered Mr. Larue. "My brother's force will see to that."

Mr. Wells commented, "You say he's a lawman, but he's against the law."

"Only against federal law," replied Mr. Larue. "State law is what we go by. Besides, ain't nobody going to know the difference if he sends a couple of his men down to the colored shacks to beat up them niggers every once in a while without arresting them, just to keep 'em in line."

"Do they actually do that?" I asked.

"Like I said, ain't nobody going to know the difference if they do or they don't," Mr. Larue said, laughing and settling back into the sofa. I guess I looked disturbed, because in an instant he sat forward again and looked straight at me, so hard I shook a little. "Now, don't go gettin' upset," he said, "Who are they protectin'? Your rights, your jobs. The other day I seen a cotton-picker machine that does the work of twenty-five nigger field hands. Where you think those field hands are going to get jobs now? If we don't keep them in their place, they'll take over what white folks have been doing. At least my brother won't have to worry. They don't allow no niggers to be cops."

They have to eat, too, I thought, but I didn't dare say it. Somehow, Negroes seemed to manage on less. I thought of Annie. She'd mend old clothes that she bought at rummage sales, take home the parts of the chicken our family didn't like, and keep her children scrubbed and neat-looking on eleven dollars a week. Nobody ever praised her ability to get by, to raise so many children with so little means. People would just sit back, shake their heads, and say, "Isn't it a mystery, how the colored get by on next to nothing."

"I guess we're best off not meddling with the situation, leaving it just like it is," said Mr. Wells. "Those big shots up in Washington don't know the truth, that our colored people are happy. Just look at them singing, dancing, loafing around. You and me ain't that happy."

"Right," said Uncle Jasper, "there's no point in messing up things as they are."

Mr. Larue lit a cigarette. "Of course, I wish the Ku Klux Klan were more active."

"Ain't likely," said Uncle Jasper, "not according to *Time* magazine." He picked up the copy that lay on the table beside him. "According to this, they've run the Klan out of both Carolinas for busting up a casino in Myrtle Beach."

"Just as well," said Mr. Wells. "I sure don't like the way the Klan takes the law into its own hands."

At that, Mr. Larue jumped up, pulled the cigarette from his mouth, and shouted, "What do you mean! The Klan *is* the law! Ain't nobody can put fear in a nigger and keep him in his place like the Klan."

Mr. Wells retreated into his chair, and Uncle Jasper searched frantically for a new subject. I was relieved to hear the front door slam and see Dad come in from the hall. I got up and moved, since I'd been sitting in his favorite chair.

"Good evening, folks," he said, as he sat down and lit his pipe. "I'd have been here sooner, if it weren't for some late-breaking good news."

"Don't know why it can't wait," said Uncle Jasper, "seeing as how you can't publish it till next Thursday, anyway."

"It was too big to wait," said Dad. "I've been meeting with the mayor and city council and a man named Philip Ingram."

The name didn't mean a thing to Mr. Wells or Mr. Larue, but it did to Uncle Jasper. "Not Philip Ingram of Pennsylvania!"

Dad nodded.

"The president of Ingram Chemical Company? Here in Peachtree?"

At that, both Mr. Wells and Mr. Larue sat erect and spoke at once. "What in the world is he doing here?"

I wondered myself. I had seen the Ingram trademark on many products. But important people just didn't come to Peachtree, with the single exception of General Lafayette during the American Revolution. Maybe we'd name a street in Ingram's honor.

"He's thinking of opening a plant here."

"What for?"

"Why here?"

Dad couldn't answer the questions fast enough. "Ingram is developing synthetic textiles now, fabrics similar to rayon and nylon. The company is working on something called Miraclon. They've chosen to locate here because labor and land are both cheap, and there's already a big textile industry in the state, so that skilled management and sophisticated equipment won't be difficult to come by. And there's plenty of power available here, because of the hydroelectric plant on Lake Moultrie."

Uncle Jasper's eyes were aglow with excitement. "You realize what this means, Garth?" he said, turning to Mr. Wells. "You realize what happens to a town when big industry hits it? Why, it'll bring people here, people who need houses to live in, stores to buy goods! They need restaurants, parks, schools, everything! And that will create more jobs for more people, and do you know what all this means? Money! Growth! Progress!"

Mr. Wells gazed dreamily at a puff of smoke from Dad's pipe. "I've always wanted to build a new store," he said. "Maybe I'll buy that property two blocks down and put in a big, modern emporium, with an escalator and air-conditioning."

"What's the timing on this?" asked Mr. Larue. "When do they begin?"

"Well, they have to complete some tests first. They'll be opening a chemistry lab fairly soon, in November."

I'd already been looking forward to November, because that month meant the homecoming football game, the selection of Miss Peachtree High, and the big dance. Now I knew I could never wait for the days to pass fast enough.

We needed a miracle for *The Peachtree News* to survive. Now the miracle was coming, and it was, appropriately, called "Miraclon."

four

"You don't have to be a salesgirl for the rest of your life."

Dad had noticed my depression. I had just spent an entire Saturday at Wells', and had made not one single sale. The dress department differed from notions, where women would happen to pass through, remember that they needed buttons or were out of white thread, and I'd ring up some small change. A new dress was a serious purchase, something few people would buy on a whim.

The department supervisor had given me instructions on how to encourage a sale. If a woman took a dress off the rack to inspect it more closely, I was to say, "Why don't you try it on? The fitting room is right over there." And then, when she came out, I was to mention the good points, compliment the woman, and perhaps suggest a scarf or piece of jewelry or shoe color to enhance the costume further.

Unless the customer was colored. "Don't suggest they try on the clothes," the supervisor had said. "They usually won't want to. But if they ask, we have to let them. Go back to the fitting room with the customer, and stay with her."

At four o'clock, as I leaned against a counter of blouses and sweaters, yawning unashamedly and wondering how much longer this interminable day would continue, a Negro woman wandered over to the clothing rack and began leafing through the dresses. I went over to her and asked if I could help. She was looking thoughtfully at a maroon dress with an artificial flower on the shoulder. She took it from the rack and walked over to the mirror, where she held it up in front of her, trying to imagine its effect.

"That should be quite becoming," I said.

"You think so?" she asked, "I can't tell. And I could use a new dress when I introduce Mrs. Westbrook to our ladies' auxiliary at the church Monday evening. But it has to be something that looks exactly right."

I sealed my lips and watched the woman take the dress off the hanger, put it against her body, turn one way and then the other. "I'm just not sure," she said, "Would it be okay if I tried it on?"

"I guess so," I said, and led the way to the fitting room. I watched as she unzipped the green jersey dress she was wearing, adjusted the attractive nylon lace-trimmed slip she wore underneath, and carefully worked her way into the maroon dress. And then I noticed with dismay that she had to struggle to fasten the buttons.

"How does it look to you?" she asked.

"The color is lovely," I said.

"Don't you think it's too tight?"

"Well, perhaps you could let the side seams out a bit."

"I don't have time for that."

"Or wear a different girdle."

"No, child, the one I have on makes me small as I'm going to get. The dress is just too tight." She wiggled out of it, handed it to me, dressed, and left, without so much as a thank you. Not that one was due. Perhaps I should have thanked her for consuming twenty minutes of the day.

The long, boring hours plus Gaston's absence for the weekend had put me in a funky mood. Mr. Wells was grooming Gaston for his future in the retail business, and had taken him on a buying trip to Atlanta.

"You ought to date someone else once in a while," Mother had suggested. How, when Gaston made it obvious that I was his girl, and everyone else had better keep away? Not that any of the other boys at Peachtree High were vying for me. Oh, well, I thought, things could have been worse. He could be gone for Homecoming, two weeks off. It was better that he be gone now.

I answered Dad's comment. No, I did not care to spend the rest of my life waiting on customers.

"She'll get married and raise a family," said Uncle Jasper.

"But even so, she should plan to have a career, just in case," said Mother. She didn't say in case what, but I knew she meant "in case she winds up an old maid."

All three looked at me, awaiting my reaction. "If I really had my choice," I said, "I guess I'd want to be a journalist."

Dad beamed.

"I am applying to Syracuse," I said. "I've already written for an application. And I'll work my way through, the way Dad did, or I'll get a scholarship or a loan."

"You know we have a little savings account set aside for your college," said Mother. "We haven't been able to add to it in the past year, but it's been earning interest, and it will help. You can live with my sister and her family, so you'll save on room and board."

"Yes, Mom, I know." I smiled, gratefully.

Dad puffed on his pipe. "If you're thinking of going into journalism, perhaps you'd like to get some experience now to see if you're really cut out for that field. The articles you write for *The Red and Gold* are fine, but I wonder if you might like to try your hand at some real reporting, for *The Peachtree News*. I couldn't pay you, but you'd get some excellent insight on what to expect."

"That would be great," I replied enthusiastically. "What can I write about first?"

"Why don't we make that your problem?" asked Dad. "Let's see what kind of nose for news you have. The deadline for your first article is Tuesday night."

That gave me three days. I thought of how little went on in Peachtree. If only we lived in Charleston or Atlanta or New York, where things were surely happening all the time, I'd have no trouble. Maybe I could write up Gaston's buying trip. I talked to him about it when he arrived home Sunday afternoon, but he didn't seem interested in volunteering information. "What are you so curious about?" he asked. "All we did was visit a bunch of wholesalers. We didn't even get to tour a factory, because they were all closed for the weekend."

We were sitting on the first floor of Gaston's screened

porch, which ran for two stories down the entire side of his house, looking out on the backyard part of the West-brook garden. Mrs. Westbrook was there, watering her flower beds. She must have heard us talking, and known that we were only a few feet away, yet she never raised her head. As she went about her yardwork she smiled and hummed a tune. I wondered how anyone could enjoy such isolation as was forced upon her.

And then I remembered that tomorrow night she would not be alone. She would be speaking at the Negro church. There was my story. I decided to mention it to no one.

I had passed the Negro Baptist church, just outside town, many times on the road to Charleston. It was three or four miles from home, and a healthier walk than I'd have attempted were I not exercising my resourcefulness as a cub reporter. The thought occurred to me that maybe there was more than one such church, so I was relieved to arrive and immediately spot the customer I had waited on that Saturday. She looked smart in a mus-tard-yellow wool dress, and was busily talking to several women at the front of the room.

The lady at the table just inside the door stared at me in puzzlement. "I'm a reporter from *The Peachtree News*," I said with some trepidation, hoping she wouldn't ask to see the press card I didn't have.

She turned to the woman at her right, who nodded. "How nice," said the first lady. "Would you like to sit up front?"

"No, ma'am, I think I'd rather sit in the back row."

The women were filing in rapidly but sitting down slowly, pausing to talk to friends. They were as well-groomed as any group of white women might be for such

43

an occasion, though their clothes looked somewhat out of style. One attractive, light-skinned woman was the last to sit down, because everyone called to her in greeting as soon as they saw her. It seemed they all had to have a word with her, if only to say, "Hey, it's so nice to see you."

She was tall, thin, and graceful, and her skin was not much darker than mine. Her light-brown hair was straight. Only a slight broadening of the nostrils gave a hint that she was a mulatto, and therefore, a Negro. She perhaps had more white genes than black, but that made no difference. A single drop of Negro blood was all it took to define the races.

Once introduced, Mrs. Westbrook began to speak with ease. She was obviously quite comfortable and at home with her audience. One by one she listed Negro rights. "All of you know that my husband protected your right to vote in the July primary. But how many of you voted?" she asked.

Not a single hand was raised.

"You have the right to use the so-called white beach out at the pond. How many of you have used it?"

Again, not a hand.

"You have the right to try on dresses in a clothing store. How many of you have ever done that?"

A couple of hands were raised, including my customer's, but she was seated on the platform behind Mrs. Westbrook, who did not see it.

"Are you going to let white people get away with the way they treat you?" asked Mrs. Westbrook imploringly. "Don't you realize that white Southerners are a sick, morally corrupt people? You do them no favor when you encourage their behavior. Remember what happened in Germany under Hitler? A whole race of people, the Jews, were almost obliterated by the Nazis. We have our own Nazis right here, in the South, even though we call them by other names. They'd like you to believe they long ago obliterated your spirit. But have they? Must you need people such as my husband to speak for you because you will not speak for yourselves?

"Will you go home and tell your men what I have said? Will you tell them you must assert yourselves, demand your rights, and bring about the true meaning of our Declaration of Independence, that all men are created equal?"

She finished, amid clapping hands and nods of approval from the audience. A child in a dainty pink dress, her hair tied in tiny pigtails all over her head, walked up to the platform and presented her with a small bouquet of flowers wrapped in tissue paper. I quietly left by the back door and began the long walk home.

I met my deadline, though I feared Dad would chastise me for my subject matter. Yet except for a few changes in sentence structure, he said he would run the story as is. He seemed pleased. I wondered if it was the chance to stir up controversy in Peachtree, or mere parental pride.

It certainly did stir up controversy. Daily papers in South Carolina picked up the story and ran it in abbreviated form. A few days later there was a story on a state senator, in which he was quoted as saying, "We ought to run that damn Yankee female across the state line."

Throughout the episodes that followed, I cringed, feeling guilty about Mrs. Westbrook and the grief I must be causing her. I would see her in the garden as I walked to and from school, making quite a fuss over her plants, never acknowledging my presence. One evening as she was out for a walk I happened to see some neighbors deliberately pass too close to her, jostling her as they went by.

Then, late one night, we were startled to hear a knock on our door. It was Gaston, quite out of breath even though he'd come so short a distance. "There's a cross burning on the judge's front lawn!" he cried. "Right now!"

We reached for our robes and went running out of the house, down the road and around the corner to where the judge's house faced out on Broad Street. But our haste was not quick enough. There in front of the big, gray Victorian house, looking eerie in the faint light of the moon, was not the first sign of foul play.

"I swear to you, it was right there!" yelled Gaston, pointing to a spot about midway between the fence and the veranda. "It ought to be headline news!"

"I can't print something I don't have facts on," said Dad. "Now, if you can tell me who did it. . . ." He looked at Gaston and raised one eyebrow.

"I don't know. I was sleeping out on the porch, on the second floor, when I thought I heard a commotion, and then saw some light above the judge's house. I ran over here as fast as I could and saw the cross, and that's when I went back and got my robe and came to get you."

We all went home. The next afternoon I searched the front yard from the sidewalk and could find no trace of anything unusual. But the word had spread. The rumor of the cross-burning was all over town. *The Peachtree News* never ran a word about it, though the week's editorial was on the meaning of a responsible press.

It was time for my second assignment. "How about Homecoming this weekend?" I suggested. "The paper always covers it."

"Nope," said Dad, "a reporter has to learn to cover all types of stories, not just those he wants to cover. I'm going to take you out to the chemical laboratory that Ingram has set up and let you write on that."

"Ugh," I said. I hadn't even taken chemistry. "Why can't I cover Homecoming?"

"Because Joe Gibbs is covering it."

"Joe Gibbs? Why him? Are you paying him for it?"

"No, but the Charleston paper is. They're letting him write it up for the sports page, and have agreed that we can run the same story, with some embellishments of interest to the local folk."

"If I were writing the story," I pouted, "I could hand it to you right now, and you'd have it for Thursday's paper, a day before the game is even played."

"Oh?" asked Dad. "That should be interesting, covering news before it occurs. How would you do that?"

"Simple. I can tell you everything that's going to happen. Sugar Moran will be crowned Homecoming Queen. She's the sole nominee of the senior class, and a senior has won it every year that I can remember. And as for the outcome of the game, we're going to romp all over Maryville, of course."

"Of course," said Dad. "Still, you never can tell. Homecoming just might hold some surprises."

Dad was speaking purely as a newspaperman. He could not possibly have anticipated what was to happen.

five

Usually I didn't spend much time dressing, but Home-coming was special. I wanted to look perfect for the dance in the gym after the game. The pink-and-brown-plaid wool skirt I had spotted at Wells' the very day it arrived lay across my bed, next to the pink short-sleeved sweater I had bought to go with it. I would also wear my white Peter Pan collar with the lace trim and a few scatter pins. I powdered my nose, blotted my lipstick with tissue, and patted the tissue on each cheek to give a faint impression of color. My hair, which I had been faithfully brushing one hundred strokes each night, glowed with a nice sheen, and though it was too curly to roll up in socks as the girls with straight hair did, it seemed to fall into place attractively just above my shoulders.

Gaston and I walked to the football field together. He didn't comment on the new clothes, only on the Tabu perfume I had borrowed from Mother. Why did he have to like the only part of my ensemble that I had vowed never to wear again? Tabu was much too heavy for me.

Gaston left me at the gate and went to join the players. He was the football team's manager, having been unable to qualify for a playing position. I located the girls with whom I usually sat. Some were dates of players and others had no current boyfriends. We usually positioned ourselves on the top row of the stands where we could feel far removed and talk about things other than football if we wished. As I looked around, I spotted Joe Gibbs two rows down, studiously writing on a note pad.

Sugar Moran was already seated on a special dais in front of the stands. She seemed especially beautiful in a dark-green suit, wearing, as did the other queen candidates, a red-and-gold chrysanthemum corsage on her shoulder.

"Lay-deez and gentlemen," the public address system suddenly blared, "may we have your attention for the start of this Homecoming celebration. We shall begin our festivities with the crowning of Miss Peachtree High of 1950."

The candidates filed off the dais and walked toward the center of the football field. Coming toward them from the opposite side were five of the players, Armand Larue in the center.

The loudspeaker continued, "And now, the moment you've been waiting for. The captain of the Peachtree Patriots, Armand Larue, will crown Miss Peachtree High . . . Miss Sugar Moran!"

Loud whoops and shouts went up from the stands as

the girls around me clapped politely. "Some people have all the luck," muttered the girl on my right.

Then the stands broke into laughter as Armand bestowed a lengthy kiss upon the new queen. The boys led Sugar and her court back to the dais, and then assembled on the field to await the kickoff.

I spent the first half of the game watching Sugar watch Armand. She was more than lucky. She not only knew how to catch Armand but how to keep him. Her grades may have been lower than mine, but she was evidently endowed with much more useful attributes than knowing the volume of spheres.

By halftime the game was tied, 7–7. Each team scored a touchdown in the third quarter, but Maryville made the extra point and we did not, making the score 14–13. It remained unchanged until the final second of the game, when Armand managed to cross the goal line for the third time, leaving us the victors at 19–14, and Armand the indisputable hero. Everyone came down from the stands and gathered between the gate and the gym entrance to cheer him as he was carried on the shoulders of the team.

The evening would have proceeded smoothly had it not been for the damaged egos of the team from Maryville. Their players, intermingled among us, shuffled along, downcast, eager to get in and out of the locker room and on their way home. We hadn't noticed that three Maryville players had broken ahead and stood at the gym entrance. Now, as Armand and his bearers approached, the trio shouted clearly,

> Peachtree, you don't have us fooled,
> Red and gold is for a nigger school!

The three dispersed quickly, but not fast enough for the Peachtree team. Armand's grin turned to a grimace. He jumped to the ground and ran after the Maryville players, back across the football field, his teammates close behind him. Joe Gibbs tore after them, pad and pencil in hand. Some of the spectators followed.

I just stood there, mulling over the jingle. Was Maryville calling us a nigger school? It didn't make sense. I felt Gaston's arm jerk mine. "C'mon," he said, "let them fight it out if they want to. I want to get to the dance."

The gym was decorated in red and gold crepe-paper streamers, and a combo of high school students played "Hello, Young Lovers" at the far end of the room. But few couples danced. We stood around in small groups, anxiously awaiting some sign that the fight was over.

It seemed much longer than the fifteen minutes counted out by the clock until our team returned. The band stopped playing as Armand entered, and we all watched him as he leaped, two steps at a time, halfway up the center of the gym stands. He breathed heavily. An angry yet resolute expression masked his face, made all the more dramatic and powerful by the grime covering his imposing figure. He surveyed the crowd and, seeing that he had everyone's attention, he said, "We're gonna change our school's colors."

A questioning murmur arose from the crowd, stilled again by Armand's voice. "That new nigger school over in Maryville, Washington High, is using red and gold."

The crowd groaned.

"We ain't gonna take no guff from Maryville High on account of it, are we?" asked Armand, speaking in quick, short phrasing, punctuated by his heaving chest. The crowd roared agreement. "We're gonna change our school colors, right?" The crowd responded with an approving whoop.

Armand resolved to bring the matter up before Student Council and asked for everyone's support, which he got from the applause and cheers as he descended the stands and walked triumphantly to the locker room. At that moment, Armand could have had anything he requested from us. But we really didn't have an alternative. There was no communication between us and Washington High, no way to ask them to change their colors, or to explain our reason.

Our first dance was broken by a concerned Joe Gibbs, who tapped Gaston on the shoulder, not to cut in, but to take me aside and talk. He led me over to the second row of bleachers, where Miss Callaway sat with the chaperones, her face set in a somber gaze.

"We have a problem," said Joe as we walked toward her. "If we change our school colors, what are we going to do about *The Red and Gold* as the name of our school paper?"

He finished as we sat down beside Miss Callaway, who picked up the conversation. "We've built a statewide reputation connected with our name. How are we going to explain if we suddenly become *The Green and Gold* or *The Blue and Gold* or"—her voice broke in exasperation—"*The Pink and Purple?*"

I thought of the entrance hallway to our school. As a visitor came into the building he saw, first, the display of a few athletic trophies we had won over the years, the newest one several years old. They were all engraved with the name of the Peachtree Patriots. Only in journalism, under the name *Red and Gold*, had we excelled. On the wall beyond the case, a row of certificates from the South

Carolina Scholastic Press Association paid tribute to our newspaper and, ironically, to the colors we were about to lose.

"That name is a symbol that goes beyond the Negro school down the road," said Miss Callaway. "What can we do to preserve it?"

We didn't know what to suggest. "Maybe if *The Red and Gold* doesn't give the issue any publicity, everyone will forget it," I suggested.

Joe added, "Armand's excited right now, and we're all feeling emotional. Maybe the whole issue will have died down by Monday morning."

"The heat will die down, but the embers will smolder until someone stirs them up again," said Miss Callaway.

We could come to no resolution. I returned to Gaston. Through the evening, as I glanced over at Miss Callaway, I noted that the expression of concern on her face had not changed.

Every so often, as we two-stepped or shagged across the floor, I would catch sight of Armand and Sugar. She had removed her corsage, and it seemed that, no matter what the beat of the number, they did the same dance, eyes closed, body against body, his arms around her waist, hers around his neck. I recalled previous years, when Sugar could not finish a dance without several boys cutting in. Now no one dared ask for that privilege.

Gaston, on the other hand, held me at a safe distance, never closed his eyes, and talked incessantly of subjects that had little to do with romance. He was planning the weekend for us. "After work tomorrow, let's go to the movies. Then, if the weather's nice Sunday, I'll borrow the car . . ."

"Nope. Sunday's out," I said, pleased that I wasn't so

readily available. "Dad's taking me out to the Miraclon lab. I'm writing a story on it."

"Aw, why can't he write his own stories?"

"I'm learning, Gaston. I want to be a journalist."

"What for? You'll just get married." This uttered, Gaston fell quiet. He must have realized he had ventured too near a subject he worked hard to avoid. "Well, anyway," he continued, "I hear it's a good movie tomorrow."

The Miraclon lab was set up four miles north of town, on a large tract of land that Ingram had an option to buy. It was a small, cream-colored building unmarked as yet by an identifying sign. The head chemist, Dr. Adams, a man about Dad's age, greeted us at the door and took us on a tour. He struck me as perhaps being a mad scientist as he strutted about the lab, showing off each facet of its operation with dramatic emphasis. He began by asking us to follow a series of pictures, diagrams, and photos along the wall. "These demonstrate how Miraclon is made," he explained. "Miraclon is a synthetic fiber produced from coal, as in this first picture, and the various chemical elements as demonstrated by this chart. They are combined and spun into threads of short length, which are combed and twisted until a cottonlike texture is obtained." Dr. Adams continued down the wall, commenting on one picture after another. Dad peered closely and listened with interest; I found myself yawning and following behind, trying to jot down enough facts to make a credible story.

"And now," said Dr. Adams coming to the end of the wall and waving his arm in a flourish, "step into the lab!"

We followed him through a door and found ourselves in a room filled with test tubes, beakers, unfamiliar machines, and several bolts of white, colored, and patterned fabric. He reached for one of the white bolts and held it out to me. "Feel this," he said, "and tell me what you think of it."

My summer at the notions counter caused me to say without thinking, "It's cotton." And then, as I picked up an end and rubbed it between my thumb and fingers, I added, "But it's so soft. Soft, even for cotton."

"This isn't cotton," beamed Dr. Adams, "this is Miraclon."

He then had us examine the other bolts, which demonstrated the variety of patterns the fabric would hold. We next followed him to a clothesline, just outside the back door, which contained four swatches of fabric. "All four of these were the same size when we brought them in here," he said. "Numbers one and two are cotton; three and four are Miraclon. One and three have not been washed; two and four have. Now what can you tell me?"

The difference was obvious. "The washed cotton shrank," I said, "and it needs a good ironing. But the washed Miraclon is the same size, and has very few wrinkles."

"Right. Now, which would you rather buy?"

"The Miraclon, unless it's more expensive."

"It is right now," he said, "but it won't be once we build the factory. We expect to turn out enough fabric for half a million garments a week."

"Wow!" I said. Dad whistled.

Back home I wished I did not have to write a long article. But Dad wanted to use it as the lead story in this week's paper, and insisted that I explain, clearly and accurately, the complete process from chemical elements to completed fabric. He read the first two drafts with disgust.

"It's dull," he said.

"The charts on the wall were dull," I answered.

"Wasn't there anything in the process that caught your imagination?"

"Well, at one point . . ." I hesitated. Dad would think my notion silly.

"Come on," he said. "At one point, what?"

"At one point it occurred to me that the whole thing was sort of like the story of Rumpelstiltskin. Remember, he was the little man in the fairy tale who could spin straw into gold?"

"Go on."

"Well, coal is even more unlikely than straw. And if the tests live up to expectations, then Miraclon will indeed be gold to Peachtree."

"Why don't you use that angle in your story?"

The lead headline of *The Peachtree News* that week was "Miraclon Plans to Spin Coal into Gold." Right underneath, I read, "by Cary Bowen." I turned to the inside of the paper. "Color War Disrupts Homecoming Festivities" by Joe Gibbs appeared at the bottom of page three.

I felt like a celebrity that weekend. Almost everyone I saw mentioned that they had seen my name. That is, everyone but J.T. Larue.

He alone sat with Dad in the parlor when I came home from work Saturday evening, and from the first words I heard I could tell he thought the paper should be headlining something else.

six

"It's the biggest story in town this week," said Mr. Larue, shaking *The Peachtree News* at Dad, "and you ain't even mentioned it."

"I've been hearing plenty of rumor," said Dad, "but not a shred of fact."

"Don't give me that," said Mr. Larue angrily. "The judge lives two doors down from you. Practically under your nose he's been entertaining niggers." He pulled out an article torn from another newspaper. "Read this. It's from a paper up in the western part of the state. And I hear other papers have picked up on it, too. But right here, where it's happening, nary a word."

Dad spoke in calm contrast to the other man's temper.

"J.T., this article doesn't say a thing. What Negroes is he entertaining? Are they political figures, or merely friends? Remember, no white man has given him so much as a charitable nod since his marriage. Could be the man's just lonely. This article doesn't say why he's entertaining Negroes, whether it's to be sociable, or to stir up racial conflict. What am I supposed to print?"

"You're the newsman. Ask the judge."

Dad stood up, walked over to the window, and looked out. "*The Peachtree News* doesn't ordinarily cover social events of this nature. The news impact of the story, true or false, is already out. At this point, I'd rather just let the matter lie."

"Bowen, you're a coward," shouted Mr. Larue. "I never thought I'd see the day when you'd be afraid to tackle something."

Dad just smiled slyly.

"Ain't much point in my staying around this evening," said Mr. Larue.

"Sorry you have to be taking off so soon," said Dad, seeing him to the door.

I waited a moment after Dad returned to the room, to be sure Mr. Larue was out of earshot. "He always starts an argument and makes things uncomfortable," I complained. "I don't know why you encourage him to come around."

Dad eased himself into his favorite chair and lit his pipe. "I need to listen to him," he said. "He represents a popular perspective in Peachtree, a viewpoint that I need to understand."

"Why? You're not trying to be like him."

"No, but among the men who sit in our parlor or on our porch most often, there is a balanced view of the way the

South Carolinian of today looks at our way of life. J.T. Larue speaks for those who would keep things as they are, at any price. He represents an extreme, but he speaks for a great many people. So does Garth Wells, although he is more moderate. He, too, wants to preserve our old Southern traditions, but he wants to do it within the law. And then there's Uncle Jasper, who represents a more liberal view. He feels the rumble of change, and knows there will be no turning back. Only trouble with him is he doesn't have the guts to speak his mind. He'll get started, and then he'll back down."

Dad sighed, and then continued. "People in Uncle Jasper's category recognize that for too long we've subjugated the colored people. But instead of encouraging black and white folks to share the same facilities, they just concentrate on making colored facilities more equal."

I recounted Dad's reasoning by summing up: "You have the bigot, the moderate, and the liberal. Every viewpoint is represented."

"No," said Dad, "it's all just shades of one viewpoint. The other side is completely overlooked."

"What's that?" I asked.

"The side that says that segregation is morally wrong."

"Why don't you ever say that in your editorials?"

Dad looked at me sheepishly. "If I did, who'd buy *The Peachtree News*?"

I mused silently, then asked, "Why don't people try to see the moral viewpoint more?"

"It isn't easy," replied Dad. "How many Negroes do you know well, Cary?"

"Annie, of course," I said, without giving it a thought. "Who else?"

"Well, I could say Willis, except I really don't know

where he lives, or whether he even has a family." I thought of mentioning Ralph, but Dad would just laugh at so limited a relationship.

"Okay, then, let's take Annie as the Negro you know best. You know where she lives, how many children she has, what she does for a living, how much she makes. Have you ever been inside her house?"

"No, I haven't."

"Do you know what makes her happy? Or what keeps her from being sad? Do you know what she might have done with her life if she could have had your opportunities? Does she dare have hopes and dreams of a better life for her children?"

I could only answer with a question. "Does any white person know?"

Dad replied, "Does any white person care?"

That started me on a train of thought I was not able to shake for several days. I reviewed all the ways Negroes were separated—in schools, in restaurants, in rest rooms, on trains, on buses, in movies, in motels.

Gaston interrupted my pondering one day as we walked home from school. "You sure don't say much lately. What's on your mind?"

How could I tell him? Then I remembered the water-fountain incident. "Remember when we were kids, back in first grade, just learning to read?"

"No."

"Don't you remember, one day we went into your dad's store, and there were two water fountains, one labeled 'colored,' and one, 'white'?"

"They're still there."

"And you drank from the one marked 'colored'?"

"I did not."

"Yes, you did. And when I asked you why, you said because it was marked 'colder'?"

"I never did any such thing."

"You did, too. I don't see how you could forget it." I realized that there wasn't much point in letting Gaston know my thoughts.

When we turned the corner on Magnolia, I was surprised to find my mother on the sidewalk, waving me to hurry. "What's the matter?" I asked, coming close.

"One of Annie's sons was hit by a car. I want you to walk her home."

"Which one?" I asked, praying that it wouldn't be Ralph.

"I don't know," said Mother, preceding me into the house. "Annie took the phone call, and it was all she could do to tell me what happened." She led me to the kitchen, where Annie sat, shaking and crying, beside the table. "Now, Annie," said Mother, "everything's going to be all right. Cary will walk you home."

We started down the long road that led behind our house, through the open fields and off to the shack where Annie lived. The only sounds were Annie's whimpers and our skirts brushing against the dry grass on either side of the way. I could think of nothing to say that would comfort her.

At the end of the road, a row of seven or eight shacks came into view. The second one in was Annie's. There was no lawn in front of these houses, just a few weeds and some scraggly bushes, all the same ocher color as the dusty yards. The houses were all of unpainted, faded wood. Window frames as well as panes were broken, and the roofs sloped unevenly down to the poles that precariously held up the porches. I often wondered if Annie ever felt bitterness at the end of a day, leaving our big, comfortable home, where the four of us had more room than we needed, and coming to her own hovel that looked as though it could not possibly hold her and all her children. When I was small, I used to imagine that a magical staircase was just inside, and that it led below to a vast underground mansion, where everyone had a separate room, just as we had in my family.

We approached Annie's yard. Some fifteen or twenty people, Annie's children and neighbors, I guessed, grouped themselves in clusters along the porch and watched as we approached. One old lady sat in the only piece of furniture in sight, a worn green rocker. She held a girl I recognized as Annie's daughter. The only sounds I heard were the rocker against the porch and, from somewhere, the hum of a church hymn.

As we entered the gate an old man, his hair white and his hands gnarled, left the porch and walked to meet us. He hugged Annie about the shoulders and held her close. In a soft voice he said, "Ernest, he gone."

Ernest. Thank God it wasn't Ralph! Which one of those little faces had belonged to Ernest?

Then suddenly I was startled by a long wail that seemed to come from nowhere and hover, detached, in the air. I turned to Annie. Her lips had drawn up into a contracted tremble, her eyes, half-closed, focused on nothing, and her whole face crumbled under the resignation of a sorrow too heavy to bear. Her body drew into a half-squat, her hands flapped uselessly in the air, and all the time she uttered this interminable wail. The people on the porch came down to her side to offer comfort, but she just moaned and blubbered, making no sense except in that universal way in which the impact of loss and loneliness comes to stay as part of a person forever.

The old man turned to me and said, "I guess you best go now. She be all right."

As I walked back down the road to our house, a vivid image came to me of my cousin's death from meningitis in Charleston in 1948. He had been several years younger than I. The disease had swept him away quickly, before we had even heard he was sick. I remembered my aunt, sitting in the living room of the house on Rutledge Boulevard, greeting townspeople and relatives who came to pay their condolences. Though Dad said she surely must be suffering greatly, she showed no sign of it. Her cordiality never faltered as she spoke of events without the slightest reference to her son, and called to the maid when it was necessary to refill the pitcher of iced tea.

"Isn't she a marvel!" I heard one visitor in the hallway say as she prepared to leave, "She's taking it real well."

And another said, "She has an inner strength."

Those words came back to me as I trod the yellow road home, kicking pebbles to one side or the other. Black people don't hold in their grief, don't even try to. But perhaps a woman who has raised nine children while doing someone else's laundry and scrubbing someone else's floors doesn't have to prove her strength when a loved one dies.

In the evening in our parlor someone said, "That's one less mouth for her to feed."

And someone replied, "I reckon she'll never miss him."

I left the room.

Annie did not return to work for over a month, until after the new year. Both Dad and Mr. Wells excused me from my part-time duties so I could do housework. Mother invested in an electric deep-fat fryer that made chicken quickly. The jars of vegetables that she and Annie had preserved were easy enough to prepare, and I soon learned to cook rice that was neither hard nor gummy. Mother and I cleaned the house together in the evenings and on the weekends. I wondered how a full-time housewife without a maid could stand the repetition of day-after-day cleaning and cooking. I was grateful for school.

No one expected any changes in enrollment of our senior class that year. The forty-five students who had started out in September would, everyone assumed, be close enough to graduation not to drop out. And the thought of a new student didn't even occur to us. We hadn't added anyone to our class since elementary school.

I was surprised, therefore, to arrive at school the Monday after Thanksgiving to find a strange boy standing by one of the pillars on the front entrance to the school, the doorway reserved for seniors. His hair was reddish blond, his skin was fair, and he had the build of football-team material, though the season had just ended.

"Who is he?" I asked as I joined the usual group of girls sitting on the far end of the steps.

"Steve Adams. Cathy Simms says he just moved across the street from her. Isn't he cute?"

Steve Adams. Why should that name sound familiar? I retraced my steps in recent weeks and remembered.

seven

The arrival of Steve Adams stirred excitement in the senior-class homeroom. The teacher introduced him by name, adding that he was, as I suspected, the son of Dr. Adams at the Miraclon lab, and had just moved down from Pennsylvania. The teacher looked around the room. There were exactly forty-five desks, one for each student.

"I'll give you Armand Larue's seat for today," she said.

I turned and looked across the room to where Armand sat, next to Sugar. Both desks were empty.

"We Southerners are known for our hospitality," continued the teacher. "I'm sure your new classmates will make you feel welcome."

Indeed we would. The students sitting around him eagerly provided him with books and checked on other supplies. The boy in front of him offered to show him to his first class.

I was delighted to find that class to be solid geometry. "The seat behind me is empty today," I volunteered, and as Steve settled himself there I felt grateful to Armand for picking such a fortuitous time to be absent.

At the end of the period I examined Steve's schedule. Darn, I muttered. He took physics, while I went to French. We wouldn't meet again until the last two periods of the day, for English and government.

Both my study halls came in the middle of the day, and I used them to work on *The Red and Gold*, which we hoped to have out by the end of the week.

Miss Callaway handed me a page to be typed on a stencil. I removed the ribbon from the typewriter, brushed type cleaner across the letters to clear any ink that might prevent the impressions from showing up clearly, and rolled the sheet in the machine. The copy already had slashes at the end of each line to indicate how many spaces to leave between words so that right as well as left margins would be even. Each line was to be typed twice to make a darker image. The finished page was proofread and initialed by three different readers. Not by accident was *The Red and Gold* the finest mimeographed newspaper in the state.

"We have a big hole on page three," said Miss Callaway, as I brought her the completed stencil. "About eight inches' worth. Too big for a filler. What can we put in?"

"There's a new student in the senior class," I said. "I could run an interview on him."

Miss Callaway nodded approvingly. "Any other town

I'd say no, but in Peachtree, that's news. Why don't you go down to the principal's office and get his background? Then you can set up a meeting with him after school."

The principal's secretary handed me his registration card. "This will give you his former addresses, birthdate, course of study, and a few other facts," she said. "Nothing very interesting."

"That's fine for a start," I said. "I'll take it into the waiting room to copy down the information."

I walked into the room engrossed in reading the card, and failed to notice that it was already occupied. I must have felt someone was looking at me; still, I jumped when I saw Armand and Sugar sitting side by side, Armand's arm around Sugar, his other hand clasped over hers. "Hey, Cary," said Armand, "how's school today?"

"Fine," I answered, "but why aren't you in class?"

He and Sugar exchanged a smug look. "There comes a time when you just don't go anymore," he said. "Right, Sugar?"

Sugar grinned.

It was an awkward moment. I wanted to say something, but didn't know what. I pretended to be studying the registration card. The secretary came in shortly and said to them, "The principal will see you now."

I copied the information slowly, hoping to be still around when Armand and Sugar came out of the office. After I took down all the details, such as the six addresses where Steve Adams had lived since he was born, I decided to write questions to ask him on a sheet of notebook paper. Still they did not come out. My interview was going to be very thorough.

At last, five minutes before the bell ending my second study hall, the door to the office opened and the couple emerged, arm in arm. They seemed quietly proud, confidently happy.

What good was my waiting? I wondered. I still didn't know what to say. But they did.

"Let's tell Cary," said Armand.

"Okay," said Sugar, giggling.

They walked over to me. Armand reached for Sugar's left hand and held it out. On the third finger was a thin silver band.

"You're married!" I gasped.

"Yeah," said Armand, "since August. We wanted to keep it a secret until now."

Sugar added, looking at her husband adoringly, "Armand just had to finish the football season."

"Yep," said Armand, "but now my school days are over and I'm looking for a job. We're going to get us a little house and settle down."

Sugar continued, "And I'm going to sew curtains and bake bread and make all sorts of little . . .oh, you tell her, Armand." Sugar was blushing.

Armand blushed, too, but the happy grin never left either face. "We're going to be a mommy and daddy."

I don't know what I said. I hope it was polite, but I felt such a mixture of conflicting feelings. I meant to say, "How wonderful!" but I was thinking, "How horrible!" And I'm not even sure why I thought that. Was it envy because this had happened to Sugar instead of me, or pity because I now knew there was more to keeping house than sewing and baking? The couple turned and walked out of the school building as students for the last time.

I never heard the bell ring, nor do I remember what path I took to the lunchroom. All I knew was that I alone possessed the hottest gossip of the whole school year. But not for long. I merely mentioned it to the girl in front of me in the lunch line, and the story spread throughout the school before the day was over.

Gaston didn't seem to care. Not since Armand and I had broken up in early summer had it ever crossed his mind that I might have liked to win Armand back. We sat across from each other, as we always did, eating beef stew and cole slaw from little compartments of our lunchroom plates. I brightened when Steve Adams sat down next to me.

I looked at Gaston. Steve had chosen to sit next to me, not him. Wasn't he jealous? He looked over at Steve and asked, "Hey, there, how are you finding your first day at Peachtree High?"

"All right, so far," Steve replied, "You're a little behind the Pennsylvania schools, but I guess I'll manage to learn something anyway."

"Guess what!" I burst out, irrelevantly. "I'm going to interview you, Steve, for the school newspaper! When can we get together?"

"How about after school?" suggested Steve.

I suppressed a chuckle. Surely that would make Gaston sit up and take notice. But he just listened, wearing his usual stupid, complacent smile.

"That's perfect," I said. "We have sixth period together (I glanced at Gaston, who had bookkeeping sixth period), so we can walk home together (Doesn't that hurt, Gaston? I'm walking home with somebody besides you) and . . . we . . . can . . . talk . . . TOGETHER . . ." It was useless. Why did Gaston assume that no other male would ever take an interest in me?

I showed Steve the way to English and later to government class. "Come," I said, "I'll show you where there's an empty seat. You'll love Miss Callaway. She's my favorite teacher."

"I hope she's not too easy," said Steve.

"Not easy at all," I replied, "You'll really learn something from her."

"I like her already," said Steve.

He spoke too soon. She stood at the front of the class, as usual, and peered at us over the rims of her glasses. "I understand we have a new student today, and I'm sure that by now you all have had a chance to meet him. We shall get on with our lesson." She then fired off a series of questions based on recent class periods and homework, summarizing what we had learned, making sure we had, indeed, learned it and were ready for today's work.

"Name the slave who was taken by his master from a slave state to a free territory and back to a slave state. Phyllis." She always mentioned the student's name last, to keep all of us at attention.

"Dred Scott," answered Phyllis.

"What did Dred Scott do, Joe Gibbs?"

"He sued, saying he was a free man."

"What did the Supreme Court decide in his case, Cary?"

"That he was a Negro and therefore not a citizen. He did not have the right to sue."

"What event in 1859 proved that the abolitionists of the North were plotting to destroy the Southern way of life? Frank?"

"John Brown's Raid."

Miss Callaway perched herself atop a desk in the front row and surveyed Steve Adams. "I don't know what you've learned in your previous school, young man," she said, "but you certainly should recognize the war that these various events led to."

"The Civil War," said Steve.

"What war?" asked Miss Callaway again.

"The Civil War," repeated Steve, more clearly.

Miss Callaway stood up and asked louder, as if perhaps Steve had not understood, "What war?"

Steve shifted uneasily in his seat. He was searching his mind for something that wasn't coming. The rest of us sat solemnly and unflinchingly. I wished somebody would say something during the unending silence.

"What war?" boomed Miss Callaway once more.

Hesitantly, Steve spoke, "The . . . War . . . Between the States?"

"Say it again."

"The War Between the States."

"That's right," said Miss Callaway, as the class let loose an audible sigh of relief. "And don't you ever forget it. Let's open our books to page two-oh-two."

The remainder of the period proceeded without incident. As I turned to Steve at the end of school he commented, "My father said the South would be different. But I didn't think they were so picky about the name of a war that was fought almost a hundred years ago. I guess they haven't gotten over losing."

"Losing?" I responded, jokingly. "We Southerners are still fighting!"

"C'mon," he said, laughing, "where can we go for a Coke?"

"There's a drugstore next to Wells' Department Store, about three blocks from here. They make good cherry Cokes."

"Cherry Coke? What's that?"

"Coke with a bit of cherry syrup, I think. I don't really know. It just tastes good."

Steve tried it. "I think I'm learning more out of school

than in school," he said, looking around. "I've never been in an old-fashioned drugstore before."

"What's old-fashioned about it?" I asked. The tiny hexagonal tiles in the floor, the ceiling fans, the small round tables, and the curved wire-backed chairs had never seemed outdated to me.

"I don't know. It even smells different. And that Wells' Department Store next door. We were in there Saturday. Is it ever an antique!"

I had been in a couple of stores in Charleston that were more modern, but I had always thought most department stores were just like Wells's. Then I remembered Gaston's dad's dream. "Once the big Miraclon plant opens, Mr. Wells plans to build a new store."

"Probably a couple of chain stores will move in," added Steve.

"Oh, I hope not," I said. "I'd hate to see Mr. Wells have competition."

"Are you kidding?" asked Steve. "Competition is the American way of life. And believe me, with the size of that Miraclon plant, this town will need several department stores. There's a big change coming to this sleepy little hamlet, and it's going to do all of you nothing but good. It's going to jolt you out of the so-called War Between the States and into the twentieth century. They'll probably level this whole block just to put some extra lanes of traffic in the road. Why, I'll bet in five years you won't recognize your hometown. It won't even be a town. It'll be a big city."

I pictured busy King Street in Charleston, then shoved it out of my mind. King Street had only two lanes. Peachtree would be much more cosmopolitan, more like New York. I tried to envision a skyscraper towering over the courthouse, with a "Wells' Department Store" sign on top. Next to it I could see an even taller building, with flashing light bulbs spelling out headlines from around the world. That, of course, would be the home of *The Peachtree News*.

"But getting back to today," said Steve, "I saw a poster in the hall at school about a hop in the gym Friday night. How about going with me?"

Without thinking, I replied, "I'll have to ask Gaston if it's all right."

"Gaston? Who's Gaston?"

"The boy we were eating lunch with."

"Oh. Are you going steady with him?"

"No." We weren't. We'd never even discussed the subject. I thought of mentioning that everyone thought of us as going steady, but that was exactly what I didn't want Steve to think.

"Then why do you have to ask him?"

"I guess I don't." I'd certainly have to *tell* him, I thought, so he'd know I wasn't going with him. But ask his permission? Good heavens, what was I thinking of? This was the situation I had been hoping for, and I had almost blown it.

"Come on," said Steve, "I'll walk you home."

It wasn't until after he had dropped me off and I had set my books on the desk in my room that I realized I had forgotten to ask a single one of the questions I had so carefully planned for our interview.

eight

I thought Gaston accepted the news of my upcoming date with Steve in extremely good grace. I didn't expect him to fly into a rage, but he might have expressed some remorse.

I waited for him on the front steps after school Tuesday, but he didn't show up. Steve walked by, stopped, and said, "I hope you're not looking for Gaston."

"No," I said casually.

"Good, because he tore out of here as soon as the bell rang. I expect he's already home by now."

"Oh."

"Now, if you'd like me to walk home with you, I'd be happy to have your company."

"Fine," I said, descending the stairs.

The week progressed with my seeing Gaston only from a distance. One morning he was just a few paces ahead of me all the way to school, yet I dared not call out to him for company.

I did feel somewhat sorry for him Friday evening, when Steve picked me up in his father's car and we drove by Gaston's house. All the way to the hop I worried about him, sitting at home alone through the long evening, plagued by thoughts of the wonderful time I would be having with someone else.

We entered the gym and found a crowd encircling one couple in the center of the floor. As everyone swayed to the mambo, the newest Latin American beat, the pair put on a lively show, moving their bodies in perfect time to the rhythm. The girl was the best dancer in the class; her date, ecstatically displaying talent he never knew he had, was Gaston. My grief for him did not give way to joy.

Gaston didn't sit down once throughout the evening. He even did the rumba and the Charleston, which I had never been able to master. Funny, I thought, that he had never shown any desire to do them when he dated me.

I couldn't sulk, though. My evening was just as successful in its way. A couple of boys, seeing that I was not with Gaston, cut in to dance with me, and though Steve then danced with other girls, he stayed by my side the rest of the time.

When we drove up to my house he asked, "Can we get together tomorrow?"

"Yes," I replied, "there are good movies in town."

"What I had in mind was your showing me Peachtree. Can we get together earlier in the day?" he asked.

"Sure," I answered, relieved that my Saturday job was temporarily suspended.

"Okay, I'll pick you up at two. Exciting Peachtree

should keep us busy until two fifteen, right?" He smiled sarcastically.

"You'd better plan on a long afternoon," I said, trying to ignore his insult.

Perhaps to an outsider there wasn't much to see in our town, but living there as long as I had, I saw a rich history in every street, every building, every tree. I pointed out the curious house on Live Oak Street that had been built just after the Charleston earthquake. Like many houses built in and near Charleston at that time, it exposed the round ends of massive bolts placed through houses to protect them from future quakes. We examined the Confederate War Memorial at the intersection of Broad and Lafayette, and I pointed out the names of several relatives who had died fighting for the South.

We took a drive out to the pond. A chill wind blew off the water, so we didn't stay there long. We then drove along the country road west of town, past farms. "My great-grandfather Bowen used to own all this land," I said. "It was a four-thousand-acre cotton plantation."

I hadn't said it to impress, especially since we didn't own it now. But Steve replied, "Your family must be very wealthy."

I laughed. It was a cynical little laugh, not bitter, but just reflecting on what might have been. "No," I explained, "when my great-grandfather died, the land was divided between his two sons, my grandfather and Uncle Jasper. A flood wiped out the plantation around 1910. They later replanted cotton, but they were never able to make a go of it again. It was attacked by the boll weevil and by taxes. And, of course, the fact that we had sharecroppers who kept a good part of the crop didn't help the situation. We lost all the land in the Depression." I shrugged my shoulders as if it didn't make any difference.

We were approaching the cemetery. "Let's stop here," I said.

"Why?" asked Steve. "Cemeteries give me the creeps."

"Oh, this one won't," I said. He pulled up beside an old oak tree laden with Spanish moss. I hopped out and walked to the cemetery gate, lifted the iron latch that kept it shut, and went inside. I hadn't been here in three or four months. My grandmother used to bring me often when she was alive; now there was no one left to place flowers on the graves so faithfully.

"Half the cemetery must be Bowen tombstones," gasped Steve, looking around.

"Oh, no," I said, "just in this section." I wandered among the stones, pointing out the granite obelisk on the grave of Great-Great-Uncle Henry, who had died a hero in 1864, and the tiny statuette above some infant cousin swept away by a plague of generations past, and the massive double slab that marked my great-grandparents' plot.

"Come on," said Steve, "Let's get out of here."

"Don't tell me you believe in ghosts," I scoffed.

"No, but it's cold, and all these tall trees are blocking out the sun. If you want to stay, I'll just take a walk outside the cemetery. You holler when you're ready." He headed to a ridge on the far side where the yellow grass was bathed in the sun.

I shivered in the cold, trying to recapture the comfort and tranquillity I always felt when I came here. The delicate black iron fence, the carefully swept paths, the tall pines and oaks, quiet except for the rustling of the wind, had, all my life, made me feel quite at home. But then I knew everyone here, through the legends that my grandparents and Uncle Jasper had told me over the years. Even my father would talk of our ancestors from time to time, though his concern was more with the present day.

And mine should be, too, I thought, as I went to join Steve, fearful of calling out from within the cemetery.

It was warmer on the ridge. He was seated and looking down the slope on the other side at a group of ramshackle little wooden buildings.

"What is that?" he asked, "a ghost town?"

"I don't know," I replied. "As many times as I've been here, I've never come over to this side of the cemetery before."

"Let's investigate," he said, walking down the slope. For someone who was afraid of graveyards, he had certainly become bold.

The buildings, four or five of them and a couple of outhouses, were huddled close together. A broken-down fence ran around them. There was hardly any space between the buildings and the fence. Steve peered into a window. "It's an old school," he said, "a deserted old school. I can see desks and a blackboard and a flag."

He then did something I would never have done. He tried the door. I would have expected it to be jammed shut with age, but it gave easily, and we walked inside. It was cold, but not musty. Ancient desks and benches stood in neat rows. Makeshift shelves around the room held old, worn books.

But not everything looked old. An open attendance book lay on the teacher's desk.

"My gosh!" cried Steve, "look at the date on the board!"

I looked around and read, "December fourth, 1950."

"That's Monday, the day after tomorrow!" he gasped. "This school is being used right now!"

I turned back to the attendance book and ran my eyes down the names. The third name down was "Brown, Ralph R." "It's the colored school," I said. "I knew there was one somewhere, but I never knew where."

"That's revolting!" shouted Steve. He headed out the door. In the schoolyard he paced up and down, looking into each of the little buildings, opening the door of one of the outhouses. "This is a school?" he asked, angrily. "Where is the lunchroom, the auditorium, the gym or the library? Where is the principal's office? There's not even a playground! The weeds outside the fence are too over-grown for the children to play out there, and there's no room inside."

Steve was so furious that I dared not voice my thoughts concerning Ralph Rutherford. This school was a good five miles from his home, yet I knew there were no school buses for Negro transportation. He walked ten miles a day to come here, and for what? The line I had seen on the book inside showed that he had perfect attendance.

Steve walked back to the car and started the engine. I climbed in, expecting him to ask where to go next. But he didn't. At first, I thought he was so angry that he just wanted to drive. But after a while I realized that he knew where we were. He was heading for the Miraclon lab.

He didn't seem angry at all after a mile or so. "I should have told you earlier," he said, "but Dad asked me to stop by the lab today. He has a new worker who is cleaning up the place. I'm supposed to make sure he's doing his work, since no one else is out there on weekends."

As we pulled in I recognized a familiar car. It was Armand's jalopy. So this was where he had found a job.

Steve preceded me into the lab where Armand, his back to us, pushed a mop across the floor. "Hi," said Steve, extending his hand as Armand turned, "I'm Steve, Dr. Adams' son. I was driving out this way and thought I'd stop in to see how things were going."

Armand wiped his right hand across his jeans and clasped Steve's. "I'm Armand Larue. And everything's fine. I ought to be through just as soon's I finish this floor." He looked over and noticed me. "Hey, Cary, what you doin' out here?"

Before I could explain, Steve answered, "My date. You two have already met?"

"Yeah," said Armand, slyly.

Steve walked back to the lab area, leaving us alone. "How's Sugar?" I asked.

"Fine. We're living in her place for the time being."

What a comedown. Armand's house in town was smaller than ours, but a mansion compared to Sugar's home. "Why don't you move in with your dad?"

Armand sneered, "You kidding? Or ain't you heard? The old man threw me out. He says Sugar's family is nothing but poor white trash."

I tried to be comforting. "He'll forget it after a while. You and your dad have always been so close."

Armand shook his head. "He ain't likely to forget. He's real mad. I wish there was something I could do to get back in his good graces."

I thought of all the arguments between J.T. Larue and my dad or Uncle Jasper. They always blew over, and sooner or later Mr. Larue was back at the house again. But this was no simple disagreement. Mr. Larue was a proud man, and he had high expectations for his family. Before Armand quit school, his dad had mentioned that he hoped Furman University would offer him a football scholarship.

Steve rejoined us. "Looks real good," he said. "We'll be getting out of your way so you can finish your job."

When we arrived back at my house, I invited Steve in to meet the family. "Won't you stay for supper?" asked Mother. "There's plenty, especially since Uncle Jasper just phoned and said he'll be at the store late. He will eat downtown. He's working on the end-of-the-year records, I suppose."

Dad snorted. "More likely, he's there because Garth wants to get the books in order for once. Uncle Jasper's bookkeeping system defies understanding. He always knows exactly where the company stands, but if anything ever happened and they had to hire another bookkeeper, the poor fellow wouldn't be able to make head or tail out of those records. And Uncle Jasper's getting up in years. He should be retiring soon."

I thought I should explain to Steve. "Uncle Jasper is brilliant," I said, "a true genius. He knows everything. You should hear him speak in Greek."

"His bookkeeping is in Greek," growled Dad.

Mother had made a shrimp creole that she served on a bed of rice. "Not a fancy meal," she said to Steve. "On weekends we have our dinner in the middle of the day. And I do hope you like Southern cooking."

"I'm getting used to it," said Steve as he tasted the green vegetable on his plate, looked puzzled, and set his fork aside, "but may I ask what you did to this spinach?"

We laughed. "That's collards," said Mother, "and you might as well learn to like it because Southerners are always eating some form of greens. If it isn't collards, it's kale, mustard, or turnips. Here, try some vinegar and hot pepper sauce on it."

Steve not only finished the collards but asked for seconds.

"Anybody who likes collard greens is a man after my own heart," said Dad, "and here I thought you were just another damn Yankee."

Those were the first kind words either of my parents had ever said about a boy I liked.

nine

Steve had dinner with us again on New Year's Day. I had dated him once each weekend during December, and was only mildly concerned by the rumor that on Christmas Eve he had taken Cathy Simms to a party.

Mother and I were working hard in the kitchen when Steve arrived. "Mind if I see what smells so good?" he asked.

"Not at all," I answered. He looked over my shoulder as I fluffed up the rice and cowpeas.

"What is that concoction?" he asked.

"Hopping John," I replied, "If you eat it on New Year's Day, you'll have good luck all year."

Though Steve ate the hopping John without complaint, as did the rest of the family, I knew it was missing something. Nobody commented except Uncle Jasper, who did so indirectly when he said, "It'll be nice to have Annie back tomorrow. I sure miss her cooking."

Annie's return meant back to work for me, too. Shopping slowed after Christmas at Wells', but the worst part to me was that the store stayed open until seven on Saturday nights. Throughout January I blamed that schedule for Steve's asking me out less frequently. A Friday-night movie was our single date of the whole month. Nothing seemed to be wrong with our relationship; he was just taking out other girls. It wasn't the kind of thing I could ask him about.

In the meantime, Gaston became more friendly, but he was dating others, too. Our only preplanned contact was lunch together on Saturdays. If we happened to leave home or school at the same time, we would walk together. No longer did we wait for one another.

The unhappiest night of all for me was the last Friday of the month. That was the Ring Dance, reserved for seniors and their dates. All through high school I had dreamed of receiving my Peachtree High School ring, a heavy gold band with a red stone, embossed on one side with a peach tree and on the other with the palmetto, the state tree of South Carolina. On the inside were each recipient's initials. The night of the dance a gigantic replica of the ring was placed upright in the center of the floor. Each couple who went steady passed through, pausing beneath the crest to exchange a ring and a kiss. On the Monday following, the boys who had received rings would come to school, wearing them on a chain around their necks, and the girls would sport their oversized tokens wrapped with adhesive tape on the inside to keep them from slipping. A few days later, professional photos of the ceremony would arrive. These would be shown around and then taken home as a reminder of the night that was, for those who participated, second only to graduation.

I had resigned myself to a long evening with a good book, *Rebecca*, and settled comfortably on the couch hoping to forget my own woes as I read of those of the anonymous heroine. Uncle Jasper was perusing a new volume he had received through the Book-of-the-Month Club, and Dad had planned to catch up on his reading of newspapers around the state.

"Did you see what Governor Byrnes said in his inaugural address the other day?" asked Dad, aiming his comments at Uncle Jasper.

"Yep. Didn't think it was unusual," was the reply.

Dad continued, "He's certainly committed to upholding the separate but equal policy."

Uncle Jasper turned the flap of the dust jacket to mark his place and set the book aside. "There's nothing odd about that. He was just reemphasizing what we all know, that we must make colored schools more equal. I expect we'll see him allocate a sizable portion of the state education budget to bringing colored schools up to par."

"I don't think it can be done," said Dad. "It will take millions of dollars, which would mean quite a tax increase. And you know who'd pay it. The whites. Colored people don't pay enough in taxes to make any difference. White people would be supporting both white and colored schools."

"Don't sound right," said Uncle Jasper. "We'd be better off leaving things as they are."

"We've done that long enough," said Dad. "Over in

Jackson County they're bringing a lawsuit because the Negro school is so inferior to the white school."

"Yeah," said Uncle Jasper, "and you can be sure some durn fool Yankee is behind it, just trying to stir up trouble. Besides, it's just one school."

"But it's representative of others," said Dad. "There's talk that this case could go all the way to the Supreme Court. Times are changing. Sooner or later we're going to have to desegregate the schools."

Uncle Jasper glanced at me, then continued talking to Dad. "You can say that now, with your only daughter about to graduate. But suppose she were just beginning school instead of finishing. Suppose the schools were integrated. That'd mean half her class would be colored. She's at an age where she's got an eye for the opposite sex, and vice versa, if you don't mind my saying so. Giving rights to the colored is one thing. But what are you going to do when some black boy wants to take your daughter out on a date?"

Dad muttered something. It was clear Uncle Jasper had won the argument. They both went back to their reading. But I couldn't concentrate on the printed words before me, not with the images that crowded them out. I pictured the ring in the school gym. I visualized a Negro couple passing through it, adopting our school's ring as their own. Then I pictured a black boy and a white girl following them. The image dissolved. The school beyond the cemetery ridge floated in before me. Maybe there was a secret door somewhere that led to a vast modern schoolroom underground. It was a silly thought, but enough to push the old school out of my mind and let me return to my book.

Business was brisker than usual at Wells' the next

morning. The once-a-year anniversary sale brought in customers from neighboring towns. I was so busy I scarcely noticed Gaston across the aisle, or Gigi, an eleventh-grade cheerleader, lingering between his department and mine. She wore her red-and-gold letter sweater. I rarely saw her in anything else. The movement to change our school colors that had begun at Homecoming had quieted down with the end of the football season and Armand's departure.

I was less concerned with Gigi's hovering presence than with Sugar Moran Larue's. She came over to a counter, fingered some blouses that had been especially purchased for the sale, and sighed, "Such a good buy."

"Maybe you could buy one and tuck it away until the baby comes," I suggested, noting her gently protruding abdomen.

"No," she replied, "I'll be needing clothes for right now and so many other things." She reached into a small bag and pulled out two patterns, one of a maternity smock and the other of a baby sacque. I pretended to admire her selection, and she, encouraged, emptied another bag of fabrics for her projects. I commended her choices, to her delight. She carefully folded everything back into the bags and left.

It was nearing lunchtime, and the store was emptier than it had been at any time that morning. I walked over to Gigi, who was leaning against a pole in the center aisle. "Is there something I can show you?" I asked.

"No," she replied, "I'm just waiting for Gaston so we can go to lunch."

Gaston? Gaston always went to lunch with me. He hadn't said a word about a third party. "Oh," I said, pretending not to mind, "that's nice that he'll have company. I'm taking a later lunch hour anyway." It was a lie that I intended to turn into truth.

"I hope you don't mind if I just stand here to wait for him," said Gigi. She self-consciously moved her left hand back and forth to show off a shiny new class ring. What was a junior doing with a senior ring? She noticed my interest and handed it to me. There was a huge wad of tape around the narrowest portion of the band, and toward the wider part, in the inside, the initials "G.W." She smiled demurely and said, "Gaston gave it to me last night."

I handed it back to her without comment and stalked across my own department, where I busied myself behind a rack of dresses, fixing belts, fastening buttons, and zipping zippers. From where I stood, I could see her through the tops of the hangers. I snapped at her like a tiger in a cage. Had she looked in my direction she might have been amused, but she was turned toward Gaston.

It's true that I was consciously wishing the ceiling would fall on her head or the floor would open beneath her feet. But I never thought to conjure up what actually did occur. Strolling toward her down the aisle was a Negro girl about the same age wearing a sweater identical in color to Gigi's. The girl brushed close to Gigi, looked her straight in the eye, and smirked. Then she sauntered over in my direction, swinging her hips in deliberate exaggeration. I watched as Gigi's wide-open eyes followed her, with an expression growing more horrified with the black girl's every step. Halfway between us, the girl turned around to Gigi and said, "What you doin' wearin' nigger-school colors, honey chile?" Then the girl put her hand over her mouth to suppress her laughter and ran out of the store.

Gigi had disappeared by the time I turned to look at her again. It was noon. I supposed I could wait until one o'clock for my own lunch. That was when Uncle Jasper usually went. He would probably be happy to have my company.

I walked up the stairs to the mezzanine at 12:55. I hadn't been there since before Annie had left in November. Uncle Jasper's friends rarely visited him on Saturdays; they had other routines to follow. Still, I had never seen his office so empty. It took me a moment to realize that the stack of ancient ledgers, normally piled on tables against a partition, was nowhere around.

Uncle Jasper was, as I expected, pleased to join me. I spent most of the lunch hour telling him my troubles. It had been a long time since I had confided in him; I had been taking my problems to Gaston. Now Gaston was one of my problems.

"You young folks nowadays are too anxious to find somebody, go steady, and get married," said Uncle Jasper.

"Oh, I don't care about that," I said. "I just want a little male company my age."

"Well, you get that now and then," said Uncle Jasper. "Take Steve Adams. He's got a level head on his shoulders. I don't suppose he went to that ring dance."

"I doubt it. He came to Peachtree High too late to order a ring, and he hasn't been dating anyone in particular. Still, if Gaston could suddenly turn up with a steady girl, anything could happen. I just can't trust men. It's enough to make me want to be an old maid."

"I used to feel that way myself," said Uncle Jasper. "I had a girl friend once and she jilted me, so I decided to become a bachelor. And you know what? Now I regret it.

If I had it to do over again, I'd take me a wife. Of course, there's a lot of things I'd do differently if I could."

"Like what?" I asked.

"I'd think about how lonesome I was going to be in my old age. My friends are dying off, Cary. And I wish I'd made more of myself; gone into business on my own. Then nobody would come along and tell me I had to quit."

"Nobody's told you that, have they?" I asked.

Uncle Jasper took his time answering. He seemed sorry he'd brought up the subject. "I don't know how to break this to your dad," he said, "but Garth Wells has asked me to retire when I turn sixty-eight next month. He wants to get a younger man in here, someone who'll keep the books so straight all he has to do is glance down them and know what's going on. Oh, I've always been able to tell him anything he wanted to know, but he says if I dropped dead tomorrow, nobody coming in new could make head or tail out of my records. That's why I've been so busy lately, Cary. I've been straightening out those books for some new fellow."

"Then you've known you'd have to retire for several months."

"No, I've known it for years. I've been afraid to think about it. Oh, I have a little pension coming; that's the least of my worries. What I dread is the loneliness ahead. When you get right down to it, I've got lots of cronies, but no real friends, nobody to talk to about all the big ideas in my head. Why, in all my life, I've never run across anybody in Peachtree who knew ancient Greek."

Someone to discuss ancient Greek would be hard to find. But there was one man who could have met Uncle Jasper at his level. It was Judge Westbrook. I wondered how the judge coped with what surely must be a lonelier and more fruitless existence than Uncle Jasper's. Sure, he might have a cause, but at the slow rate of change in Peachtree, he would never live to see it come about.

ten

When Uncle Jasper retired in February, he spent about a month in Charleston visiting my aunt. After he returned, he settled into a pattern not much different from the one he'd had at Wells. His friends would visit him often at home, or he'd read, or walk downtown to his club and play chess.

Meanwhile, Dad studied the newspaper's circulation and income figures in recent months. They showed a continuing decline. We had an elated interlude when he sold an article about Miraclon to *National Weekly*, one of the most widely read magazines in the country. The check helped a little bit during the cold winter months. We knew it shouldn't take much longer for the preliminary tests at the Miraclon lab to be completed. Then new residents would come to town and circulation and advertising would rise rapidly. There was no more talk of letting Annie go. We would soon need her more than ever.

From the end of January to the first of April, I counted only a handful of dates with Steve. Cathy made sure I knew about every date she'd had with him. I kept a secret tally, figuring we were about even. Mother said there was nothing wrong with his not being ready to settle down with one steady girl, but I felt if he were truly fond of me, he would forget anybody else. He perplexed me. I liked him more than any boy I'd ever known, and he seemed to enjoy my company.

Thus winter passed rather gloomily. But spring brought new hope. I received a letter of acceptance from Syracuse University, and Mother's sister wrote to say I was welcome to live with them, and that they were looking forward to seeing me again after all these years.

I greeted the first warming trends in Peachtree with optimism. The bright, fresh days of early spring forced the lawns and trees to sprout new greenery, and the tender blossoms of azaleas burst forth in red and fuchsia glory on every well-kept lawn in town.

No lawn was prettier than the Westbrooks'. The bright colors stood in sharp contrast against the forbidding gray house. Annual flowers of countless variety sprouted in merry borders around the colorful bushes and along the walkways. Each day some new bud seemed to discover its ability to blossom forth. I thought it a shame that everyone in Peachtree passed by this house in such a hurry, missing all its beauty. I made up for their haste by lingering as long as I could.

The pace of my life quickened in April. The planning of graduation activities, still two months away, began in earnest. We received our schedule of end-of-the-year events, decided on a class gift, and ordered caps and gowns.

"We'll be the last class to wear red and gold," said Gaston the day we tried on our gowns for size. Gigi's incident at Wells' had brought renewed demand for change.

"Like heck we will," interrupted Joe Gibbs. "When the vote comes up next month, we'll turn it down. The whole *Red and Gold* staff is against it, and we have a lot of influence. Right, Cary?"

"We'll sure give it a fight," I said, pushing my arm through the sleeve of the gold gown that Peachtree High girls traditionally wore. I couldn't tell Joe that our side didn't stand a chance, not even after the persuasive editorial he had written. The truth was that nobody read the editorials. In fact, since *The Red and Gold* had eliminated the gossip column because it lowered our score in statewide competition, no one read much of *The Red and Gold* at all.

A boy spoke up. "I feel funny about wearing red already," he said. "Do you suppose those Maryville niggers might have their graduation ahead of us, and we might be wearing the same gowns they wore?"

The representative of the cap-and-gown company, who had been listening, spoke up. "What will your new colors be?"

"Green and gold. None of the schools we play has those colors."

The representative said, "If you'll give me two weeks notice, I can see that you have your green-and-gold gowns for graduation."

Cheers went up from the class. I glanced at Joe. The outcome of the vote seemed predetermined.

The bell rang, indicating time for lunch. We hurried to finish.

Cathy hailed me to sit down with her in the cafeteria. She then called out to Steve. That way, she could inject into the conversation the fact that she was dating him Friday night. Then she quickly switched topics. "Isn't it exciting, being a senior? We're always missing class for one thing or another."

"Yes," I agreed, "and we'll miss next period, too."

"Why?" asked Cathy.

Steve knew. "Haven't you heard? President Truman fired General MacArthur, and today the general is going to make a farewell speech before Congress. It's a history-making event. We're all going to get to hear it."

"How can we do that?" asked Cathy.

I couldn't help but enjoy her ignorance. "Silly," I said, "through our new P.A. system. The principal just hooks it up to the radio, and it will be broadcast in every class."

"Isn't that amazing, what modern science can do!" exclaimed Cathy.

Steve sneered. "In Pennsylvania, we've had a P.A. system for years."

At the start of fifth period, we all sat, books closed on our desks, attentively waiting for the speech to begin. The public address box sputtered and snapped, and some boogie woogie music came on. The class snickered as the box went dead. When it came back on, General Mac-Arthur was already being introduced.

The class settled back, certain that anything the general would say would be remote to our own experiences. He spoke of people in Asia, halfway around the world. World War II had left them in a state of poverty. They needed food, clothes, housing. But there was something they yearned for even more. MacArthur spoke of it in phrases such as "the realization of the normal nationalist urge for political freedom" and "the dignity of equality and not the shame of subjugation."

No, we never felt such needs as these. Not us. But we had neighbors in our same town who did. The millions of black Americans could understand the Asians, because they lived through the same experiences. I looked around the room. Some class members were doodling, some were passing notes, some had their eyes closed. Did no one else see the connection?

The speech was ending. "I now close my military career and just fade away—an old soldier who tried to do his duty as God gave him the light to see that duty.

"Good-bye."

The class yawned and stretched audibly. The teacher, seeing that there was still time left in the period, assigned homework on relative pronouns. There was no attempt to discuss the speech.

But I thought of it as I walked home alone. Why didn't people understand each other, when they lived so close? Yet who was I to speak? I remembered Dad's question of several months ago. "How many Negroes do you know well?"

And then I began to wonder. Could we ever know anyone well whom we could not regard as equal? If there was always a barrier that said one group of people was inferior, how could we ever hope to meet its members on common ground?

The Westbrook house loomed before me now, and I paused at the fence to see if I could spot any new blooms. A rustle came from the azalea bush closest to me, despite the fact that there was no wind. Perhaps a dog or other small animal was crawling through it. I waited and saw nothing, though the rustling continued. Maybe the animal was stuck. "Hey," I called, leaning over the fence and sweeping back some branches, "does somebody down there need help?"

"Oh!" came a voice from the other side, and up popped Mrs. Westbrook, her face even with mine, scarcely an arm's stretch away. Her amazement at seeing me could have been matched only by my own, and for an instant we stood facing each other in openmouthed astonishment. When she finally recovered, she asked, "What did you say?"

"Nothing. I just thought something might be stuck in there, and wondered if I might help get it out."

"Oh, there is, my dear. It's a dreadful weed. Why don't you come through the gate and see if you can get at the root better than I can? You're much more slender, and might be able to squeeze back in the bush farther. Here, I'll give you my gardening gloves so you won't dirty your hands."

I saw no graceful way of telling Mrs. Westbrook "No." Besides, I didn't have to worry about being seen on Westbrook property, since there was no one in sight and I would be down behind the bush anyway. I slipped in through the gate and donned the gloves.

The weed was tougher than I expected. "Beware of the thorns," warned Mrs. Westbrook, as I gingerly grasped a barren part of stalk and groped around for the root with a trowel. At length the plant gave way, and I pulled out a long and scraggly weed.

Mrs. Westbrook was full of gratitude. "Why don't you come up on the veranda, and let me reward you with some iced tea I just made a while ago? And I also have a lovely treat, some date bars, homemade by my sister in Boston." She paused and waited expectantly for my answer.

My first instinct was to refuse. On the other hand, I reasoned, what was wrong with accepting a gentle neighbor's hospitality? I thought of all the "society" people in town who at one time or another had probably received a similar invitation, and had declined. Why should I add to Mrs. Westbrook's hurt?

"I can't stay long," I said, as if to indicate a middle answer between "yes" and "no."

"That's all right," said Mrs. Westbrook, "Come and sit down while I pour us both some tea."

I chose one of several freshly painted white wicker rockers comfortably cushioned in a pink floral pattern, and surveyed the world from the Westbrook veranda. The garden was just as pretty from this side, revealing flowers this side of the bushes that I hadn't seen before. Now and then along Broad Street, someone hurried along, not noticing that I observed them.

Soon Mrs. Westbrook came out with a tray bearing tea, sugar, lemon, and date bars. She set it on a table between us. "One teaspoon of sugar or two?" she asked.

I dared not say three, the luxury I allowed myself at home. "Two."

We sat, sipped, and nibbled for a minute or longer. I was happy to have my mouth full, since I didn't know what to say.

Mrs. Westbrook broke the silence. "I wondered for a moment there, when I asked you up, if you'd be like the others. But I knew you were different."

What did she mean by that?

"I know who you are, Cary Bowen. And I knew the night I saw you at the church, sitting alone there among all those Negro women, that you were a decent person. Fine article you wrote on it, too."

I thought back to the article. And I remembered the trouble it had stirred up for the Westbrooks.

She continued, "And knowing your father is the editor of the paper, I was surprised he sent you out on an assignment like that."

"He didn't," I said, gulping down a last morsel of date bar, "I thought up the idea myself."

Mrs. Westbrook clapped her hands together. "How marvelous! Well, then, why don't you write more articles like it?"

"I just stumbled on the subject," I explained. "Normally, I never know what's going on in the Negro community."

"Why, all you have to do is ask me," she said. "I know everything that's going on. But then again, maybe you're like most of us. You're young yet, even if you are a newspaper reporter. Maybe you just don't feel comfortable among strangers, particularly Negro strangers. Am I correct?"

"Yes, ma'am. I guess so."

"Well, then, I think I know a solution. Why don't you come to dinner some night? How about the second Friday in May? Yes, that would be good. It will give you a chance to learn a few things that will help you understand Negro ways. And isn't that the key? Don't we feel more comfortable among people whom we understand?"

Had Mrs. Westbrook been following me in my thoughts all day? Could she read my mind? The second Friday in May was the night of the Junior-Senior Dinner

Dance. The invitations had already gone out, and I hadn't sent or received one. But how would she know that?

"That's awfully nice," I said, "but I wouldn't want to put you to any trouble."

"Nonsense. I'd love it. I'll expect you here between seven thirty and eight."

eleven

Dad was on the phone when I came in. I didn't notice any excitement in his voice as he spoke, but when he hung up and joined Mom and me in the parlor, he could not contain himself. "Listen, everybody," he announced, "that was Barkley Higgins, editor of *National Weekly*, calling long distance from New York!"

"Wow!" I said. "What do they want?"

Dad replied, "You remember the article on Miraclon, which I sent them unsolicited and they bought? Well, they liked it so much that now they're assigning me an article!"

"Terrific!" said Mom.

"What's the subject?" I asked.

"The segregated school case over in Jackson County."

I was puzzled. "Why that? Why would the whole country consider it important?"

"It may well be a landmark decision," said Dad. "Judge Westbrook will be one of three federal justices called to rule on that case sometime in early summer. If either of the other judges is as liberal as he is, the case could put an end, once and for all, to segregated schools. And if it doesn't, the case will go right up to the Supreme Court of the United States. It's likely the separate-but-equal doctrine won't stand much of a chance against those northern sympathies."

The phone rang again. Dad answered it. This time his mood was definitely one of disappointment. "No! That's awful!" he said. "What happened? I'll be right out there."

He came back in the parlor just long enough to pick up his pipe. "I've got to go," he said.

Mother pleaded, "Can't you tell us what's going on?"

Dad paused. "That was Dr. Adams from the Miraclon lab. He wanted me to be the first outsider to know. The Miraclon lab is closing."

I cupped my hand to my open mouth.

"Why?" asked Mother.

"Something about the fabric not standing up through tests," he said. "I'll find out the details when I get out there. Then I'll let you know."

But he couldn't let me know. When he came home he went straight to his typewriter, where he worked on into the night. When I awoke for school, he was sleeping. Steve was my only hope for information. Maybe he wouldn't know yet. But he did; I could tell as soon as I hinted at the subject.

"I'll drive you out there this afternoon and show you the problem," he said.

The lab was hardly a hubbub of activity. Only Dr. Adams and Armand were there, sorting through equipment and packing it in boxes. Steve led me out the back door to the clothesline, which now held about a dozen fabric samples. "These swatches have been out here for three months, in cold weather, rain, and heat," he said. "Look at them, feel them, and tell me what you think."

I felt the first one, silky smooth. "Nylon," I said, and Steve nodded. The next was similar, though it had a rougher texture. "Rayon?" Again, a nod. I continued down the line, identifying other fibers including Miraclon, the swatch on the end.

"What big difference do you notice?" Steve asked.

"Except for the color, no difference," I said. "All the fabrics are white, except the Miraclon, which is sort of an uneven brown."

"All the fabrics were white when they were first hung out," said Steve, "but Miraclon is heat-sensitive, and turns brown in the sun. Come on inside and I'll show you something else."

We walked to a corner of the lab where an ironing board was set up. Steve plugged in the iron and clipped a piece of Miraclon from a bolt. He ran the iron, which had barely time to get warm, over the cloth. The fabric disintegrated.

"Isn't there anything you can do about that?" I asked.

"Nope," said Steve, "they've tried everything. The company has called Dad back to Pennsylvania to work on a more promising product."

"Then I guess you'll be leaving right away."

"Not till after graduation. Since that's only a few weeks away, Mother and I will stay here. She'll take her time packing, and then we'll head north."

We walked out to the entry area, where Armand was

dismantling the wall display. I remembered how I'd hated those charts and photos when I first saw them; now I felt a pang of sorrow at seeing them go.

Dr. Adams stood at the reception counter, looking quizzically at a pile of a dozen bolts of white Miraclon. We greeted them both. "How's Sugar?" I asked Armand.

"She's coming along real well," he replied. "The doctor says the baby will arrive in early May."

Dr. Adams snapped his fingers. "I'm glad you said that, Armand. Here I've been looking at this stack of Miraclon and wondering what to do with it. I'll bet Sugar could use it for diapers. There's so much of this stuff, all she'd have to do is cut it to size, use it once, and throw it away. Can you imagine that? Disposable diapers! What will I think of next!"

We laughed. Armand's expression brightened. "Those will come in handy, especially if it takes me a long time to find another job."

"You won't have any trouble," said Dr. Adams, "not with the good recommendation you'll get from me. Come on, Steve, let's help Armand carry these bolts out to his car."

There was nothing else we could do to be of help, so we drove back home.

Uncle Jasper was sitting in the parlor. "So you're dating the Adams boy again," he said, as I walked in.

"Some date," I said. "I initiated it."

"A date's a date," said Uncle Jasper, not looking up from his newspaper. "By the way, you'll be eating alone tonight. Your parents are working late at the paper. My club is having a dinner for a member who's leaving town and moving to Florida. Annie will fix your supper."

I walked back to the kitchen, past the dining table, set

for one. Annie was just readying her own meal on an old chipped china plate she always used. She laid it at her place at the kitchen table. "I'll give you your meal now," she said.

I twisted uneasily as she ladled out my portion from each pot, allowing her own supper to get cold. "How you been today?" she said, handing me the full plate.

"Fine," I said, and took the plate into the dining room. But instead of sitting down, I picked up my silver and napkin and brought them back into the kitchen, where I placed them beside Annie. Then I sat down and began to eat.

Annie said nothing.

"You asked me how I've been today," I said. "The answer is more than just 'Fine.' If you really want to know, I can't very well tell you from the dining room."

Annie piled some peas onto her fork and chewed them in silence.

"I've had a lovely day," I continued. "I had a date this afternoon with Steve Adams. We went for a nice, long ride. Now. How have you been today?"

Annie said nothing. She stuffed a forkful of food into her mouth and washed it down with iced tea.

"How are your children? How is Ralph Rutherford? I haven't seen him in ages. He must be a big boy by now."

Annie rose, some food still left on her plate. She went to the sink, cleaned her dishes, and continued about her work.

I did not try to sit with her again.

twelve

Sugar's baby girl and the *National Weekly* with Dad's story both arrived in Peachtree on the first weekend in May. Somehow I squeezed in time to read the article, but my present for the baby took more effort. Since Sugar appreciated handmade things, I decided to embroider three bibs with the baby's name. But so far, only one bib sported the pink letters S-H-A-R-O-N. The other two were proceeding slowly.

Other things kept me busy, like studying for final exams. I had qualified as salutatorian, an honor, I suppose, except that it meant I had to write a speech. Yearbooks arrived, meaning every senior had to have the autograph of every other senior. And there were parties for the whole class.

And if that weren't enough, we had to vote on changing the school colors. It didn't take up any time, other than being a topic of conversation, or being just one more thing to think about.

We filed into the auditorium one day to listen to advocates for either side. Gigi spoke first, recounting her tale of horror and shame that day at Wells' when a colored girl had humiliated her. I muffled a snicker as she spoke.

Next came two football players. They warned that other rival schools could pick up the cheer Maryville High had yelled at us. The audience clapped vigorously at their every pause.

Then came the incoming president of the Student Council. "We must never let anyone interfere with the pride we have in our school," he said. The audience roared approval. "What is color? What difference does it make whether we wear green or red? In a few years no one will remember that we once used red and gold. But if we still have the same colors as Washington High, we'll always be open to a lot of heckling."

Joe Gibbs was called as the next speaker. He carried a stack of small boards, which I instantly recognized as the plaques we had won over the years, which hung by the trophy case. An emotional quiver ran through his voice as he said, " 'What is color?' asks our last speaker. I'll tell you what color is." He held up one plaque after another, shaking an angry finger at the writing. " '*Red and Gold*,' it says here, 'awarded first place for excellence as a scholastic newspaper.' *Red and Gold, Red and Gold*. Would you wipe out a reputation known throughout the state? Are all these honors for nothing?"

He sat down. Someone from the audience added an amendment to the main motion, changing the newspaper's name to *The Gold and Green*, with small letters underneath saying, "Formerly *The Red and Gold*." The ammendment passed overwhelmingly. I glanced over to Miss Callaway, who sighed in resignation.

I thought the speeches were surely over now. But one final speaker was announced, Steve Adams. What could he possibly say that would add to the other presentations?

He leaned on the podium in a relaxed manner and looked around, catching the eye of several students in turn. "I think you're making a big fuss over nothing," he said. "Somewhere in the state there must be a colored school that uses the colors green and gold. So what? I'm sure all of us know how to handle teasing. Ignore it and it stops, right?

"Let me ask you a question. How many of you own red-and-gold sweaters?" About half the hands in the audience went up. "Now, those are expensive sweaters. What are you going to do with them? Are you still going to wear them? Are you going to pass them on to someone else who doesn't know about this little dispute? Or shall we bundle them into a package and send them over to Washington High?"

A few people laughed. Maybe he was getting somewhere.

"Does anyone know why we have the colors red and gold?" Steve asked. Not a hand was raised. "I haven't lived here as long as the rest of you, but I can answer that. Of all the colors readily available in sweaters, uniforms, pennants, and the like, red and gold are the closest to that of a peach. I asked a neighbor who remembers when the colors were adopted. He feels you're ending a fond tradition. So think twice before you make this change."

"We want change!" shouted a voice several rows behind me.

"Get that damn Yankee out of here!" hooted a boy across the room.

Steve raised his hand to try to regain the audience's attention, but it was no use. The whole school seemed to break loose in verbal insults. The moderator asked Steve to sit down, and with a careless shrug of his shoulders, Steve returned to his seat.

Six students voted against the motion, Steve, Joe, and I among them. "That's five more votes than I expected," said Steve in government class after the vote was announced.

"Surely you knew I'd vote against it," I whispered.

Steve beamed. I wouldn't have thought how I voted would make much of a difference to him.

I caught up with him at his locker after the final bell. "I don't understand why you spoke at the meeting at all," I said. "You made a lot of enemies, and the outcome surely can't matter to you."

"My side had to be heard," said Steve, "I tried to tell the students by stating reasons they would understand, rather than going into my real conviction in the matter."

"What is that?"

"Just that people, regardless of color, are people. It isn't red and gold they're upset about; it's black and white."

I watched Steve walk away alone. For him I was glad that Miraclon was closing; he had certainly alienated himself in this community.

I, too, walked home in silence. The day's events made me glad to be leaving Peachtree High.

I sulked all afternoon, but when supper came, I could see that Dad was in an unusually good mood. He seemed anxious for the rest of us to sit down and get settled.

"I have an announcement," he said.

We all put down our forks and looked at him. Dad savored our bewilderment for a moment and then asked, "How would you like to move to New York City?"

I gasped, "I can't imagine living anywhere but in Peachtree."

"Then maybe it's high time you did move," said Dad.

Mother interrupted, "You're not just making idle comments, dear. What's on your mind?"

Dad put down his fork and spoke. "With the Miraclon lab closing, *The Peachtree News* will continue to decline. The only way to keep it going is to deprive ourselves of every luxury and, eventually, necessities. I can see the day when a newspaper in this town will not be profitable at all. We might as well face the fact and get ourselves a better situation now."

"Have you tried the *News and Courier?*" asked Uncle Jasper.

"No," replied Dad, "I decided to go another route. When I sent in my second article to *National Weekly*, I also sent along a résumé and asked for a job. They wrote back with an offer, and have invited me up to discuss it with them. I could start in mid-June, which means we'd all move up just after Cary graduates. And speaking of Cary, it will be nice to have her live so near Syracuse University. If we kept on living here, she'd only be able to come home once a year, at Christmas. But if we're living in New York City, she'll be just a little more than two hundred miles away." He paused and asked, "Well, what do you think?"

Uncle Jasper wiped his mouth with his napkin and shook his head. "Not me. I had enough of the North in college. I can't take the cold winters. Besides, I'm too old."

But Mother was enthusiastic. "I think it's a wonderful

opportunity! Many times over the years you've said that you wished you could have stayed up North. And I'd love to live closer to my family. Now we have a chance! And even though you're over forty, you still have more than half your working years ahead of you."

Dad turned to me. "How do you cast your vote?"

After this afternoon's experience, I was glad to be voting with the winning side. But I really did feel an excitement about the whole idea.

Dad concluded, "Now the whole thing isn't definite, because there are a few loose ends to be tied together yet. So let's not say a word of it on the porch tonight."

We didn't. There were plenty of other things to talk about. A half dozen men joined us that evening. I had finished my homework, but was feeling too lazy to work on the bibs.

Even J.T. Larue, whom I hadn't seen in months, was there. The early arrivals settled themselves comfortably in the rocker, the armchairs, or the porch swing; the later ones sat in the upright straw-seated chairs or along the porch steps, where I usually sat out of courtesy to my elders. No one seemed to realize that over the years I had matured enough to be entitled to one of the chairs.

I thought everybody who was coming was already there until I heard Uncle Jasper say, "Well, look here who's coming up the street."

We all turned to see Armand's jalopy rounding the corner by the judge's house. J.T. Larue bristled at the sight of his son. "What's he doing in this part of town? It's a sure thing he's got no business at this house."

But Mr. Larue was wrong. Armand parked and came up our walkway amid a flurry of congratulations. He smilingly accepted them until he caught sight of his father who sat, arms crossed in front of him, mouth clamped shut, looking off in another direction.

In a soft voice Armand stated his purpose. "Mrs. Bowen asked me to come by when I had a chance to pick up a present for the baby."

Mother opened the screen door long enough to hand Armand a gift wrapped and tied with a pink bow. "I have to apologize," I said, catching Armand's attention. "I'm making something for the baby, but it isn't finished yet. I'll take it over to Sugar as soon as it's ready."

"Sugar will be plumb tickled with something you made yourself," said Armand.

He seemed in no hurry to rush off, and glanced anxiously in the direction of his father.

"Sit a spell," suggested Uncle Jasper. "You're grown enough now where you can come around and visit us on an evening."

Armand sat on the top step across from me. His eyes fastened upon his father, who was determined to look away.

"And you, J.T.," said Uncle Jasper, "you're grown up enough where you can speak to your own son. He's just made you a grandfather. And you know what I hear around town? That you haven't even been to see that new granddaughter of yours. Why, you'd think he married a colored girl, the way you carry on."

J.T. Larue snorted, "He should've married a nigger. Then I could have him arrested."

Armand pleaded, "Aw, c'mon, Dad. You don't mean that. I'm your own son." But Mr. Larue acted as though he didn't hear Armand's voice.

We sat in silence for a moment, each of us searching for something pleasant to say, with the exception of Mr.

Larue, who seemed bound to start an argument. " 'Course I don't know why I'm sitting on this porch anyway," he said at last. "Bowen, I know you were right fair in that article you wrote on the Jackson County school case, but it sure gripes me, sitting here only two houses away from that . . . that . . . I won't say it, there's a lady present."

I looked around, wondering who she was, then realized he meant me.

"Did you notice how fast Governor Byrnes reacted to all the publicity?" asked Uncle Jasper, veering the conversation into a more agreeable direction. "He's announced that if segregated schools are abolished, South Carolina will abolish public schools."

"How can he do that?" I asked.

"He'll make them all private," said Uncle Jasper. "He has a plan to lease out the public school buildings. It sounds kind of drastic, and I don't know that it'd be acceptable to the federal government. Maybe they ought to try one mixed school somewhere and see how it works."

Mr. Larue slammed his fist down on the arm of his chair so hard we all jumped. He stood up and shouted angrily, "Don't you know God intended for the races to be separated? Can't you accept God's will?"

God? I wondered. Did he mean the same God who created all men equal?

Mr. Larue continued, "Are you all too blind to see that's why He put the white man in Europe, the red man in America, the yellow man in Asia, and the black man in Africa? It was His way of telling us He didn't want 'em mixed up." Mr. Larue stalked down the front steps past Armand and me and turned toward us. His fist was

113

clenched and his eyes glowed with wrath as he spoke. "So old Judge Westbrook is gonna rule in favor of the niggers in this Jackson County case, huh? I tell you, that man's crazed with power. There's nothing I'd rather see than that judge run out of town."

He did not wait for our response. He turned and walked off into the night.

thirteen

It was the second Friday in May.

The full moon was already high in the sky, clear and pale above the gray-pink clouds, as I walked to the West-brooks' house. I entered through the gate on Magnolia Avenue and walked around the veranda to the front of the house so that people who passed on Broad Street would not notice.

Mother and Dad knew I was going there. They seemed pleased. No longer was there any need to conform to what everyone in Peachtree expected from everyone else. Just in knowing we were moving north, I felt that I had joined a much larger world.

Mrs. Westbrook met me at the door. I had not noticed

before how pretty it was, a heavy glass panel beveled at the edges, etched with a graceful design of a maiden dipping an urn into a stream. The door opened into a hallway, just as many old South Carolina houses did, with all rooms to one side or the other. Mrs. Westbrook led me into the living room. "Make yourself comfortable, dear," she said. "I'll get you something to drink."

I sat gingerly on a couch, a dainty period piece with gracefully curved wooden legs, unlike our overstuffed slipcovered sofa at home. The room reminded me of one I had seen in a world-history book of a European palace. Two gold cabinets enclosed with glass, displaying an assortment of trinkets, flanked either side of the white-mantled fireplace. A porcelain clock, painted with delicate flowers, rested on the coffee table before me, its ornate hands pointing out the exact minute to which I had set my watch before leaving home. Four gold balls on the base of the clock acted as a pendulum, rotating first in one direction, then in the other. A china dish of salted almonds and a footed silver compote of mints were also on the table. Why had I chosen the one seat in the room nearest the food?

Across the room I noticed, on the windowpanes facing Broad Street, an etched design similar to that on the door, but smaller. Behind me was the dining room. I turned toward its wide entrance to see, beneath a gracefully curving candelabra, an elegant table set with a lace cloth and a centerpiece of flowers from the garden. And then I noticed what should have struck me from the first. The table was set, not for three, but for seven.

At that point my observations were interrupted by Mrs. Westbrook. "I'm so sorry to have kept you sitting here by yourself," she said, carrying in a tray and handing me a ginger ale from it.

Behind her walked a tall, thin Negro man, dressed in a well-tailored suit. Mrs. Westbrook introduced him. "Cary, this is our houseguest, Dr. Cleveland Dorman. He is president of a small Negro college in Florida."

An equally slender, well-dressed black woman entered the room. "And this is his wife, Mrs. Dorman," continued Mrs. Westbrook. "The Dormans are on their way to Philadelphia, where Dr. Dorman will deliver a paper at a meeting."

"I'm happy to meet you," said Mrs. Dorman. "Mrs. Westbrook is so kind to put us up for the night. Otherwise, we would have had to drive straight through."

I was surprised. Surely a college president could afford a hotel room along the way.

"We're just delighted to have your company, Mrs. Dorman," said Mrs. Westbrook, "and we look forward to your staying with us on your way south again."

"Oh, we couldn't possibly. That would put you out too much."

Mrs. Westbrook was about to protest, when I interrupted, "There's a lovely guesthouse in town, just one block off Broad, on Cypress Street."

Everyone turned to me. They smiled politely, but no one said a word. Then I remembered. The guesthouse, like every place of overnight lodging I knew, accepted white patrons only. A sweat of embarrassment flooded through me.

"Nonsense," said Mrs. Westbrook to Mrs. Dorman, mercifully ignoring the fact that I had said anything at all, "I insist that you stay here. The room will be prepared for you and waiting."

The twilight in which I had walked to the Westbrooks' had turned to darkness. I found myself wondering if we would ever eat this evening, though the nuts staved off my hunger to some degree. Unfortunately, the bowl was empty. And no one had been eating them but me.

The doorbell rang. Mrs. Westbrook answered it and led in two more guests, a dark-skinned man and a light-skinned woman. "This is the Reverend and Mrs. Cook," she said. "I'm so glad you could meet our houseguests, the Dormans. And this is Cary Bowen. Perhaps you've noticed her byline in *The Peachtree News*."

"Indeed I have," said the Reverend Cook, extending his hand to me, "but I hadn't expected you to be so young. That is a compliment, isn't it?"

It took me only an instant to remember that I had seen Mrs. Cook before. She was the mulatto at the church the night Mrs. Westbrook spoke.

"The judge won't be able to join us until dinnertime," said Mrs. Westbrook. "He's in the library, studying the Jackson County school case."

The phone rang, and Mrs. Westbrook excused herself to answer it in the hall.

Dr. Dorman said, "I imagine the judge has his hands full of decisions now. There are so many changes taking place around us."

"Yes," said the Reverend Cook, "but you know, I rather like things as they are. We no longer feel threatened by the Ku Klux Klan; we haven't had a lynching in ages. Things are proceeding quietly and smoothly. I think we would do well to love our brothers, black or white. That way, our people won't get hurt."

Just then we heard Mrs. Westbrook's voice from the hall. Up to that point, she had been listening to the person on the other end of the phone. Now she answered, slowly and calmly. "You must be a terribly sick person to call just to tell me such nasty things," we heard her say. "Haven't you anything better to do?"

Dr. Dorman shot a sharp glance at the Reverend Cook. "Are our people the only people who shouldn't be hurt?"

Mrs. Westbrook returned, as happy and unruffled as before the phone call. "Let's move to the dining room," she said. "I'll call the judge to join us and tell Jennie we're ready to be served."

The judge entered and sat at the head of the table. In turn, he spoke to each of the guests. When he came to me, he said warmly, "Well, Cary Bowen! You've certainly become a young lady since last we spoke. Do you remember how, when you were a little girl, you used to come to the back door and ask Jennie for cookies?"

"Yes," I said, laughing.

"And one day, you showed up with a big sign around your neck that you proudly showed me. It said, 'Please Do Not Feed!' "

I didn't remember the sign, probably because I was too young to read, but my mother had told me about it. Well, Cary Bowen hadn't changed in respect to her fondness for food. I would try to remember that and not wolf down everything tonight.

We ate a meal that combined Jennie's Southern cookery and Mrs. Westbrook's New England favorites. There was a crab bisque, roast beef with Yorkshire pudding, spinach, parslied potatoes, and corn bread. For dessert we had lemon-meringue pie.

At the end of the meal Mrs. Westbrook offered cordials to her guests, except for me. Judge Westbrook said, "Cary, you're too young to drink and I don't care to. Why don't we excuse ourselves and catch up on old times?"

I followed the judge into the library. "I really had another purpose in coming back here," he said, winking. "The Reverend Cook is rather wishy-washy in his attitude toward giving Negroes the rights they deserve. I thought perhaps Dr. Dorman might be able to challenge him a bit, make him see how he's holding his people back. It's something of a paradox. The Reverend Cook wants to do the right thing. Yet I can't make him see that he is doing the wrong thing by encouraging the breaking of federal law."

I remembered back through the years, when another Mrs. Westbrook had inhabited this house. I replied, "I suppose people do change. You certainly have."

"Yes, Cary. Perhaps you'd like to know why."

I nodded vigorously.

The judge walked over to a window and stood before it, his back to me, and spoke, "Before I was appointed to the bench, I didn't know any Negroes. Oh, sure, I knew them in a sense. I knew Jennie and the other maids I've had through the years. And I knew laborers. They were always regarded as inferior creatures, and I never really thought much about their feelings.

"But when I became a federal judge, I began to see all sorts of inequalities I'd never noticed before. I remember a white lawyer calling half a dozen witnesses, 'Mr. Jones,' 'Mr. Smith,' and so on. It wasn't until he called a black witness that I noticed something different. 'Jeb Watkins,' he said, 'Jeb, you here?'

" 'Yas, suh, I is,' said Jeb Watkins, and he took his place on the stand. That lawyer kept his witness on the stand quite a while, but never once did he refer to him as 'mister.' I thought all along that perhaps they were old friends, but I found out, at the end of the trial, that they'd never laid eyes on each other before that day. That's just the Southern way. Do anything you can to avoid lending a colored man any dignity.

"And the more I thought about it, the more illogical

things became. For example, a colored man can be a postman, but he can't be a cop. A colored man and a white man might be permitted to work side by side on the same job. Then again, depending on a lot of meaningless factors, they might not. None of it made sense."

The judge walked over to a library shelf, pulled out a thick volume, and started leafing through the pages, talking all the while. "So I started reading. And I learned I wasn't the only one who felt this way. I read books by W.J. Cash, Lillian Smith, Gunnar Myrdal. I learned that a Negro family's average salary is less than a third of a white family's. But even if they have the money, colored people are limited in how to spend it. Movies are segregated; so are restaurants and most recreational facilities—if not by law, then by custom. So we see them singing, talking, or just loafing. And we say, 'Look at the happy Negro. He doesn't need much to make him happy.' Wrong! He doesn't *have* much to make him happy!"

He passed me a huge and heavy book, the one by Gunnar Myrdal. "The whole country has been talking about this book," he said, "but you won't find a copy in the Peachtree Library. Feel free to borrow it any time."

He eased himself into a heavy leather chair. "Of course, reading wasn't the end of my own self-education on racial injustice. After I'd read all I could, I began to visit Negroes. Just sort of at random, some here in town, some in Charleston. I'd meet them in court and say, 'Mind if I drop by and see you sometime?'

"And they'd look at me like I was daft and say, 'Yas, suh, boss. You come on by.'

"And that's just what I did. When I drove up, all the neighbors would come out on their porches and look at me, and once I was inside the house the children would peer at me from around the doorjambs, and my host would shift uneasily from side to side.

"And then I'd leave. But I'd come back the very next night. The second visit, the neighbors didn't take so much notice, and the family, seeing that no harm had befallen them from my first call, relaxed and talked freely. Soon I saw that their concerns and feelings weren't much different from my own. And I left with an ever-growing conviction that no matter what color we might be on the outside, we're a bunch of pretty similar souls on the inside."

The judge finished up, "Well, that's the story of an old man's change of heart. That's how a likable, respectable citizen turned into a cruel, vengeful, crazy fool."

"But that's not true," I protested. "Why, you have more feeling and understanding than any other person I know."

"That, Cary, is because you've taken the time to listen to me, just as I listened to those families I visited. You know, almost everybody has a good reason for doing as he does. You just have to take the time to listen to him."

"But doesn't it bother you that everyone in town hates you?" I asked.

The judge smiled and slowly shook his head. "I don't hold any importance to how they feel. What does matter to me is that I'm satisfied with my life. I have a clean conscience, and, best of all, at the age of sixty-eight, I have a cause to live for."

"But what about the ostracism and the threats?" I asked.

"Ostracism doesn't bother me. I have plenty of friends. See that stack of mail on my desk? It's from people, black and white, all over the country, who agree with me. Only here at home am I regarded as a lunatic. As for the threats, what can anyone possibly do to me at my age that can matter?"

I didn't want to think of the possibilities.

"Tell me, Cary, how do you feel about desegregated schools? Desegregation will not come easily, and you'll be carrying on this fight, on one side or the other, long after I'm gone. Who's going to help Peachtree adjust to this new life? It won't be easy."

"I don't expect to be living here," I said. I hadn't planned to tell the judge about our moving, but I knew, since he stood apart from the rest of the community, that the secret would go no farther.

"It's a good move," said the judge, "one I've been contemplating myself."

He noted my surprise and continued, "It's time I retired, and I will, just as soon as I finish a last piece of business. The Jackson County school case could be the most important one of my life, and I intend to see it through. But come, we've kept away from the others too long. Let's rejoin them in the living room."

He led the way down the hall and we joined the rest in the living room. The conversation had turned to little, unimportant things. I was enjoying myself.

At one point I thought I heard footsteps outside. I looked at the others, but no one seemed to notice. Then I heard them again, closer, at the front of the house. Just as everyone else seemed to notice, too, we heard a crash. Through the etched glass window, a missile hurtled toward us. Instinctively, we all ducked, then fell to the floor. The object landed just beyond the sofa and skittered across the dining room. There was a loud noise like a gunshot, then another.

Then all was quiet. We lay on the floor, not daring to breathe. Slowly we looked around. No one was hurt; nothing but the beautiful window was damaged. I searched out the thing that had come flying through. It was a brick.

The judge began to crawl toward the hall on his hands and knees. "Be careful!" said Mrs. Westbrook, "they can spot you through the glass door."

He made his way to the telephone table and crouched behind it for protection. "Get me the FBI office," we heard him tell the phone operator.

He waited a long minute, then hung up. "The office is closed," he said, "There's no way I can reach them until Monday morning."

"Call the police," I suggested.

"Ha!" The judge laughed, and for an instant I chided myself for a stupid suggestion. But perhaps it was not so dumb, because that's what the judge did next. "They'll send someone right over," he said to us. "At least that should be good for some documentation of what's happened."

It was a good twenty minutes before a single policeman arrived at the door, inquiring, "What seems to be the trouble, Judge?"

The judge replied, "Our house has been attacked." He pointed to the object on the floor.

The policeman walked over, picked it up, and said, "It ain't nothin' but a brick."

"It could have killed us!" cried Mrs. Westbrook.

"We heard shots!" I added.

The policeman shrugged his shoulders. "No need to get hysterical. Weren't nobody hurt. I'll file a report on it."

He turned to leave and we followed him to the door. Only then did we discover a lone familiar figure standing in the darkness by a pillar of the porch. I jumped, but so did he.

"Gaston Wells!" I shrieked. "What on earth are you doing here?"

"Is everything all right?" asked Gaston.

"Seems to be now," said the judge, "but why are you here? Did you see anything?"

"I heard shots," said Gaston. "I was lying down on the sleeping porch when I heard them, and I thought I better investigate. I got up, grabbed my robe, ran down the back stairs, and just as I got to the door I saw, rushing past . . . aw, shucks, you'll never believe this."

"What did you see, Gaston?" I asked, impatiently.

Gaston's eyes widened as he said dramatically, "The Klan!"

I looked at him skeptically. "There's no Klan in these parts anymore," I said, "Are you sure it wasn't a ghost? That's just as likely."

"Now you know I don't believe in ghosts," said Gaston.

"How many Klansmen did you see?" asked the judge. "And which direction did they go?"

"I don't know how many," he replied, "All I saw was one. He ran right through my backyard and then headed toward the Bowens'. I guess from there he took off through the open fields."

"Why did you wait so long to tell us?" asked Mrs. Westbrook.

"Scared, I guess," said Gaston, "I haven't been to this house for years. In fact, if I hadn't spotted Cary coming over here earlier this evening, I probably never would have come by."

"Gaston," I said, "tonight is the night of the Junior-Senior. How come you're not there with Gigi?"

"Aw, we had a falling out. I just don't understand women," he replied. "Well, I better be going back home, seeing as how everything appears to be all right."

"Do you suppose there really were Klansmen?" asked Mrs. Westbrook after Gaston left.

The judge replied, "It's unlikely."

I remembered the burning cross on the judge's lawn, the cross no one had seen but Gaston. "Yes, it's quite unlikely," I added.

But why would Gaston make up such stories? Could this be the same Gaston who for so long had been my best friend? He may not have understood women, but neither did I understand him.

fourteen

I hadn't expected to find anyone still awake at my house when I returned, but they were all sitting at the dining-room table, going over a stack of papers. I wanted to tell them about my evening, but my mother's worried face put me off from the subject for the time being.

"How do you move from a house you've lived in for twenty years?" she asked, "We'll have to sell the news building, and find a buyer for the press and other equipment. There is so much to do."

"It will all get done in its time," said Uncle Jasper.

They sat, poring over papers and making lists. At last, Dad remembered where I had been. Once I told them all that had happened, they wondered why I had hesitated to say anything.

Between the events at the judge's house and the thoughts of moving, I couldn't sleep. I slipped out of bed, found the baby bibs, and finished them. Pleased with myself, I planned to deliver them the next evening after we got back from Charleston.

I was awakened too soon by Mother. "Hurry, we need to get an early start to be in Charleston when the stores open," she said.

We had many errands to accomplish there. I needed shoes and a white dress for the graduation festivities that did not require a cap and gown. A Charleston jeweler had offered a gift of a sterling-silver pin in the shape of a spoon to each girl graduate. The pins were in all the popular silver patterns, and were engraved with "1951" on the inside of each bowl. Since my own marriage was too remote for me to select a pattern I anticipated collecting, I chose "Buttercup," a floral design that I knew I would enjoy wearing.

That trip took most of the day. By the time I returned home, ate the midday dinner Annie had kept warm for me, picked up the bibs and walked the distance to Sugar's house, it was already dusk. Sugar sat in a rocker in the living room, the baby in her arms. Some of her family members, all female except one small boy, were seated around her in worn, rickety chairs or on the slipcovered couch. An odor of beef stew wafted in from the kitchen, where I heard faint conversation.

"Do sit down a spell," pleaded Sugar. "Surely you don't have to rush off. Danny, get up and offer my friend Cary your chair. You know you oughtn't be sitting when there's a lady standing."

Sugar passed the baby to a sister to hold as she excitedly opened my gift and held up the bibs, each one separately. "And you did the embroidery yourself! Oh, Cary, I didn't think you sewed! And Sharon's name is on each one! See, Sharon, that's your name!"

The bibs were passed around the room so that family members could examine them and compliment my meager attempt at handiwork.

But one member was missing. It was too late on a Saturday afternoon for Armand to be working.

Sugar took the sleeping baby back from her sister, held her close to her breast, and rocked her. "We were just talking about the old days, at Peachtree High," she said. "I would be graduating with you in just one more week."

She made the statement so ruefully that I tried to offer comfort in my reply. "Yes, and most of us will become housewives and mothers just like you, whether we receive a high school diploma or not. You just have a head start on the rest of us."

Sugar smiled, but her expression soon turned to one of sadness. "Do you remember the night of Homecoming?" she asked.

"I'll never forget it," I replied.

Sugar continued, "It was the happiest night of my life. There I was, in the middle of the football field, the queen of the whole school, knowing that Armand Larue loved me, knowing that I had his baby in my belly to prove it, that Armand had chosen me for his wife. I thought life would go on and on like that moment, that my happiness would last forever. But it didn't, did it?" She paused.

"You still have Armand, and now the baby," I said.

"The baby is all I have," she muttered. "As for Armand . . . it hasn't been easy for him, I know, moving in with my family, helping with everybody's bills. But still, with his baby barely two weeks old, you'd think he might stay home."

"Where is he?" I asked.

"Heaven only knows." Sugar sighed, "He has a new job, but he still ought to be home by now. It's his second night out in a row."

Sugar's sister interrupted. "We think he has another woman."

"Oh, no," I said, not wanting to believe it. "He's probably just out seeking some male companionship, someone he can have a beer with and discuss politics. In fact, just a few nights ago he was over at our house, sitting on the front porch, visiting my uncle and my dad."

Sugar shook her head in despair. I stayed a while longer, spending more time there than I wanted to, for I saw no way I could gracefully excuse myself. Finally a child appeared from the kitchen and announced, "Supper's ready. Cary, Momma wants to know if you're planning to stay."

"We've plenty," said Sugar. "Momma makes enough for Armand whether he's here or not."

"No, thank you," I said, and left. The food smelled hearty, but after my late dinner, for once I wasn't especially hungry. I hurried back home. That night I slept soundly.

The next morning I found that the day before there'd been a great flurry of activity at the judge's house. Word of the brick-throwing had got out, and newspaper reporters and photographers had been eagerly hunting stories there. The *News and Courier* sent a reporter to our house Sunday afternoon to ask me questions about the incident. Dad secured a promise that I would be mentioned as "a visitor" rather than by name, which could cause trouble for me at school. I told the man what I knew, thinking it strange to be answering questions rather than asking them.

A photographer took pictures of the broken window and the brick. There was no explanation for the shots. Perhaps they had been fired into the air as a scare tactic.

As soon as the FBI learned of the incident, they posted a twenty-four-hour guard at the judge's house. A team of investigators uncovered nothing. Gaston stuck by his story, but with no Klan organization in the area, and no trace of anyone having run through our yards, there seemed little the federal agents could do to follow through.

At first I was keenly aware of the guard's presence each time I turned the corner of Broad and Magnolia. But after a day or two I forgot he was there, and life proceeded as usual.

Soon after, Dad went to New York to finalize his job offer, and even rented an apartment for us in Queens, just a short subway ride from his new office. I listened with excitement to his description of life there.

Now we could tell the whole town we were moving. Mom's relatives wrote to invite us to Syracuse on the first weekend possible.

Exam week began. Uncle Jasper was rocking on the porch when I came home from my English final. "We've good news," he said. "We've sold the house."

"Sold it?" I asked. "Oh, Uncle Jasper, I thought you'd live in it."

"Nope. I'm going to Charleston to live with your aunt. Never thought I'd see a time when there wouldn't be a Bowen left in Peachtree, but it's come to pass."

I started to go in the house. "I'd be careful in there if I were you," said Uncle Jasper, a twinkle in his eye. "There are two wild women inside."

The "wild women," I soon found out, were Mother and

Annie, nervously wrapping our enormous ancestral collection of silver, china, and crystal in newspaper, and placing each separately wrapped piece into a sturdy bin.

"You're excused from this today," said Mother, a tired look etched around her eyes. "Tomorrow, when you're finished with exams, you can pitch in and help Annie while I go down to the newspaper office and tie things up there."

The next afternoon I made up for my lack of manual labor the day before. Annie took charge and barked orders.

As I carried one large basket of trash out to the garbage cans I heard a scuffle behind me and a low voice say, "Hey! Cary!"

I turned and was startled to see Gaston. He pushed aside the bushes dividing our driveway from his house and came through. But once in full view, he stood awkwardly, as though he regretted signaling me at all.

"What is it, Gaston?" I asked.

"I can't believe you're leaving," he said. "I always thought you'd be right here, next door, where I could confide in you if I ever needed to."

"Confide!" I said, indignantly. "Why, Gaston Wells, you've hardly said a word to me for months."

"Maybe so, but there sure have been times when I wanted to talk to you. Like when Gigi would be sulking or mad, and I just couldn't understand her. I wanted to come over here and ask how I could get in her good graces again. I needed, well, sort of a sister to explain such things to me."

I glanced at his finger, the one where his ring would have been had Gigi ever given it back. "It looks as though you haven't had too much trouble figuring her out for yourself; I mean, after all, you are still going with her."

"True," replied Gaston. "She never stops speaking to me for more than a few days, and then it's always, 'Oh, Gaston, I can't live without you.' I expect we'll get married someday, when I finish college."

"I'm happy for you," I said. "The Bowens may be leaving Peachtree, but I guess the Wellses will always be here. You'll be running the store one day, and you'll probably build a nice little house."

"Oh, I won't be building any houses. Dad's bought yours. He has it all figured out that he'll rent it until I get married and can move in."

"My house!" I cried. "Why, that's wonderful! I mean, you'd take good care of it, and respect it, and remember that the Bowen family owned it for generations before . . ."

"For crying out loud," interrupted Gaston, "we're buying a house, not a monument! I don't mean to hurt your feelings, Cary, and I'll always remember you, but your house will have a future as well as a past."

I chided myself for my sentimentality. But perhaps I was not the only one pressed with nostalgia. Gaston's gaze fell beyond me, and when I turned, I realized he was staring at the door to the secret stairway. It stood there like a forgotten part of the house, tucked in behind the willow tree. "Remember the fun we used to have there as kids?" he asked.

"Yes. Maybe your children will some day play there like we did," I said. "Maybe they'll even dream up the same ghost stories we did."

"Come on," he said, walking over to the door and yanking it open, "let's climb up the stairs once more, just for old time's sake. We can hide from the world just as we used to do."

He left the door open so that a little light came in, enough so we could find the bottom stairs. Then we worked our way up to the landing, just outside the laundry room. There our feet became tangled in something soft.

"What's this?" asked Gaston, as we sat down in the darkness.

"Probably some sheets," I replied. "I guess Annie stuck them out here to get them out of the way. The house is such a mess, she probably didn't have room for them anywhere else."

"They sure are better than sitting on the hard wood," said Gaston.

We sat and recalled all the pleasures of our childhood, reverting to the silly ways we had acted then. It was as though we had entered a time machine and had stepped back a dozen years. We might have stayed there forever, had we not heard Annie's voice through the door from the kitchen. "Now, where is that girl? I sent her out almost an hour ago to empty the garbage and I ain't seen her since. Young folk these days got no responsibility."

"Oops," I said, "I'd better be going." We dusted ourselves off and parted casually, not wanting to believe that we would never feel so close to each other again.

fifteen

Graduation was at three o'clock on Tuesday, the movers were to arrive Wednesday morning, and we would start our drive to New York as soon as they left. The disarray in the house tended to make everything take twice as long. I could not find my white dress, which I was to wear beneath my gown and then later to the party at my home-room teacher's house, nor could I find my spoon pin. After a frantic flurry, Annie found the dress on the back of the kitchen door where she had hung it after a final pressing, and Mother found the pin, already packed away.

Somehow, we managed to get ready, and Mother, Dad, Uncle Jasper, and I arrived at school. I headed for Miss

Callaway's room, which the girls were using to put on their caps and gowns. As I pulled on my rented gold robe I felt grateful that, unlike the boys, who wore green, I was garbed in the color that had always belonged to Peachtree. But what difference did it make? I thought, as I hooked it down the front. Soon I would be leaving, and Peachtree High, regardless of its colors, would be a part of my past. A long time might go by before I walked these halls again. Perhaps forever.

I heard a sniffle behind me and turned around to find several classmates close to tears. "These were the happiest years of my life," said one, "and now they're over."

"How do you know?" I asked. "We're on the threshold of adulthood. Anything can happen."

"For you, maybe," she said. "You're moving away to a big city. But we're just staying in Peachtree, and I'll be just like my mother, and raise a bunch of children who will go to Peachtree High. That is, if I'm lucky enough to get married. If I'm an old maid, I'll have to live with my sister the rest of my life."

She said no more. We were being called to line up single file according to our height, as we had practiced in rehearsal. We left the room and joined the boys' line to form a double row at the entrance to the auditorium. The first strains of "Pomp and Circumstance" signaled the couple at the head of the line to start the slow march down the aisle. As I waited my turn I glanced at the boy next to me. We had shifted so much during rehearsal that I forgot I had been finally paired with Steve.

"Are you going to the party afterward?" he asked.

"Yes," I said.

"Can I take you?" he asked.

"Yes," I whispered, just as the couple ahead of us

moved through the entrance and we took our first step. Mother commented later that I had never looked more radiant than on that brief walk to the stage.

The ceremony went quickly. Diplomas came in keepsake folders, the certificate in the bottom half, and a drawing of our school above. One more item to pack, I thought. The girl next to me opened her folder and choked back a sob.

Steve and I did not stay at the party long. "It's disgraceful that I feel so aloof," I said as we drove away. "For eighteen years these people have been my whole life, and now it's as though I have graduated, not just from school, but from an inferior level of existence."

Steve chuckled. "You'll feel back at that level again just as soon as you get your bearings in New York."

Dad greeted us at the door. "I didn't expect you home so early, Cary. Why don't you both come in?"

Steve followed me. "Things are crazy at my house, too," he said, noting the barrels we had to weave around.

We walked back to the kitchen, where Annie was laying a stack of linens, neatly ironed and folded, on the table. "I'm all caught up with the wash," she said.

"You did remember the sheets out on the landing behind the laundry room, didn't you?" I asked.

"What sheets you talking about, child?" asked Annie. "I done did everything I know of."

I opened the door from the laundry room to the stairway. The sheets that Gaston and I had discovered on Monday still lay there. Annie and Steve followed behind me. "Law', child," said Annie. "I ain't never put no sheets out there. I ain't used that staircase in years."

"Well, they had to get here somehow," I said, stooping down, gathering them up, and separating the pieces. "I guess it's not so much for you. Just one sheet and one pillowcase."

I held up the smaller of the two pieces. Annie shrieked and fell against the wall. "That's not a pillowcase," said Steve. "It looks like a ghost costume."

I turned the piece around to see a hood, with two round circles cut for eyes. "No," I said, "not a ghost. The Klan."

"How did a Klan outfit get in your house?" asked Steve.

I just shook my head. "Maybe Gaston really did see a Klansman that night," I said. "But who knows about the staircase? Just my family and his and . . ."

Something about the feel of the fabric prompted me to plug in the iron that stood upon the board in the laundry room. It was still warm from Annie's use, so I only waited an instant before applying it to the cloth. As I lifted the iron, the fabric, as I suspected, disintegrated.

"Miraclon!" gasped Steve.

My mind was unraveling facts quickly. "Steve," I said, "think of everybody who could possibly have had Miraclon in his possession the night the judge's house was attacked."

"Easy," replied Steve, "just one person: Armand Larue."

"Oh, Steve," I asked, "what should we do? I know why Armand would do what he did. He didn't intend to hurt anyone; he just wanted to scare the judge to get into good graces with his father again. He isn't really guilty."

"He is guilty," said Steve, "and from what I read, the brick could have hit someone in the head. How would you like that to happen to you?"

I shuddered, remembering that it almost had.

"It isn't our place to decide Armand's fate anyway,"

said Steve, "but we shouldn't withhold the information. Why don't we walk over to the judge's house and tell him what we know?"

I tucked the sheet and hood under my arm and we left. "Don't bring that thing back here,"Annie called after us.

I had never thought I would visit the judge again. He examined the sheet with interest, and then called his wife and the guard to see it. The guard took down particulars, Armand's age, vocation, and address. "You seem to have this case pretty well tied up," said the judge, "even to the fact that the Larue boy wasn't at home that night."

"I hope things won't go harshly with him," I said.

"The law will deal justly," replied the judge in a reassuring voice, "and it might be, when this whole thing comes out in the open, that his father will see the situation in its true perspective."

Mrs. Westbrook added, "I like the fact that the Wells boy involved himself. Perhaps they aren't such bad neighbors after all."

"I had wondered about that myself," I said. "The only thing I haven't been able to explain is a cross he claims he saw burning in front of your house one night last fall."

"Oh, that," said the judge. "As soon as I saw it I went out, snuffed the flames, pulled it from the ground, tamped the dirt down around it, and brought it inside. I didn't think anyone else had seen it, and we decided to keep the incident quiet. There was certainly never a word of it in the press."

Mrs. Westbrook disappeared into the kitchen and returned with a plate of cookies and a pitcher of iced tea. "A little farewell party for our old friend, Cary, and our new friend, Steve," she said. "Let's sit down in the living room and enjoy it."

It really is a farewell, I thought, as I spooned sugar into my tea. And it was appropriate, for of all the people I might see no more, it was these three whose company I had come to enjoy the most. Tomorrow morning Steve would be on his way to Pennsylvania, and we would be leaving soon after.

Steve and the Westbrooks had taken an immediate liking to each other. "Cary never told me she had such a handsome beau," said Mrs. Westbrook.

Steve blushed. "I'm afraid I haven't been much of a beau," he said. "I have too many years of school still ahead of me before I settle down, so I've never even thought of becoming too sweet on one girl." He sipped his tea and looked across to me. "In fact, Cary, with exams and moving, I haven't spent much time with you lately at all. I don't even know what your plans are once you move to New York."

"I'll go to college in the fall," I said. "The same school my dad attended. It's upstate, about two hundred miles from New York City."

Steve said, "I hope you're talking about Syracuse University."

"I am," I said. "Why?"

"Because," he replied, "that's where I'll be going."

Author's Note

Though most of this book is fiction, Judge Westbrook and his wife are based on people who really lived. Their true life counterparts were Judge and Mrs. J. Waties Waring. He was a federal judge residing in Charleston.

The Jackson County case referred to in the story also had a real counterpart—the Clarendon Case, which has a further history. In July of 1951, with Waring dissenting, a three-judge federal court ruled that the doctrine of separate but equal schools should be upheld. It was carried on to the United States Supreme Court, to be heard with similar cases. One of these was *Brown* vs. *Topeka* which, in 1954, became the landmark case beeedeclaring school segregation unconstitutional.

People look back on Judge Waring today and say he was born too soon. I prefer to think of him as a man for his time, for without such courageous leaders, the future he anticipated might never have come about.